Given

KELLI MAINE

[illegible] novels
e not [illegible] Maine
astinating on [illegible] dishwash
ound avoiding [illegible] most time o
gically planning her vacation requests to get the most time o
convincing herself she doesn't really want that dark chocol

Find h[illegible]

headline
ETERNAL

Published by arrangement with FOREVER
An imprint of Grand Central Publishing

First published in Great Britain in 2014
by HEADLINE ETERNAL
An imprint of HEADLINE PUBLISHING GROUP

1

Cataloguing in Publication Data is available from the British Library

ISBN 978 1 4722 1130 9

Offset in Garamond Light by Avon DataSet Ltd,
Bidford-on-Avon, Warwickshire

Printed and bound by CPI Group (UK) Ltd, Croydon, CR0 4YY

Headline's policy is to use papers that are natural, renewable and recyclable products and made from wood grown in sustainable forests. The logging and manufacturing processes are expected to conform to the environmental regulations of the country of origin.

HEADLINE PUBLISHING GROUP
An Hachette UK Company
338 Euston Road
London NW1 3BH

www.headlineeternal.com
www.headline.co.uk
www.hachette.co.uk

To families in their many shapes and forms

No one lies so boldly as the man who is indignant.

—Friedrich Nietzsche

Acknowledgments

As the Give & Take series rounds out with *Given* and *Take This Man*, I'd like to extend my sincerest gratitude to a wonderful editor, Lauren Plude, who reached out to me with enthusiasm when *Taken* was in its infancy and had the vision and guidance to see Rachael and Merrick's story through two more novels and two more novellas. Because of Lauren, Amy Pierpont, and Emmanuelle Morgen, I've had one of the most thrilling experiences of my life so far: seeing my books on bookstore shelves. Thank you for that! It's been a pleasure working with the Forever team on the Give & Take series.

The biggest champions an author can have are book bloggers and reviewers. I've had the amazing opportunity to meet so many crazy, book-loving, dedicated women who blog for the sheer joy of interacting with other readers and authors. These women give up time from family and friends to spread the love of books. In August 2013, I was a host and organizer of The Naughty Mafia Rocks Vegas, and I was blown away by the bloggers who pitched in to help set up and make sure the signings ran smoothly. Four bloggers who joined in the planning and organized their own signing as part of the events deserve more than thanks for everything they do for the reading and writing community: Christine with Shh Mom's Reading, Holly with I Heart Indie Books, Jennifer from Wolfel's World of Books, and Ellie with Love N. Books. We couldn't have done it without you guys! A special thanks to Andrea Gregory for running the Facebook group for attendees, answering Facebook messages, and being the Café Press shopkeeper—these are huge jobs to take on and we appreciate your help a ton! Aimee Pachorek, Keelie Chatfield, and Susan Sunderlin, thank you for always being supportive and wonderful! Chasity Jenkins and Donna Soluri, I'm excited to see what the future holds. Onward and upward!

Being an author is very similar to strapping in on the world's biggest roller coaster. There are highs that are insanely high, and lows that make your stomach bottom out. One constant is the support and encouragement of my family. I couldn't write without my mom who thinks I can do anything and rushes over to give me pep talks when I need them; my dad whose words in college when I was working two jobs, interning for free and going to classes full time, "Buck up and do it," have stuck with me and become my motto; my sister who's always ready to rush in and face an army of adversity for me if she has to; my husband who instinctively knows when to give hugs or tough love (a.k.a. a kick in the ass); and my two funny, quirky, amazing kids who are old enough now to understand why they can't read mom's books and are still proud of me anyway!

My biggest thank you goes to you, the readers who have reached the end of Rachael and Merrick's story with me. There will be new characters and stories to come and I hope you enjoy them as much as the Give & Take series.

Given

One

Merrick

Sleep wouldn't come to me. I was no stranger to insomnia, but this was different. This was sleeplessness due to frustration and worry.

Countless hours had been spent racking my brain—where was Nadia? I'd left my daughter several messages and hadn't heard from her in at least a month. All I wanted to do was make sure she was okay and taken care of.

I padded down the grand staircase, barefoot, into the open, three-story entryway of Turtle Tear Hotel. Moonlight lit upon the wall murals, wavering with shadows from the trees outside the windows. It made the painted birds seem to move in that eerie, hallucinogenic way of sleepless midnights.

I should be in bed, curled up against Rachael. It wouldn't be long before she woke and came looking for me. Causing her worry was something I hated, but staying in bed, staring at the ceiling, had driven me mad. I had to get up and move.

Taking quiet strides down the hallway, I exited through the patio door. The fountain gurgled. Water fell from the conch shell the stone mermaid held in her hands. Frogs called from the banks of the island. I'd love nothing more than to feel the cool grass between my toes and breathe in the breeze off the water, but I knew it was too risky to walk that close to shore at night in the Everglades.

Sitting in one of the wrought iron patio chairs, I slouched down and looked up at the moon. It was hard to believe that not long ago, I stood in this very spot—the hotel behind me still in ruins—and was the loneliest man on the planet. Now that I had Rachael and my family, my son, Nadia's twin, MJ, nothing was going to take them away from me.

I took a deep breath and held it in, fighting off the foreboding feeling that this happiness was fleeting. As I blew it out, the soft, deep notes of a cello reached my ears from the direction of the boathouse.

I chuckled. Beck playing the cello was as likely as Beck becoming my best friend, but there it was—both recent facts. Lately, everything that had once seemed absurd and impossible was happening.

I threaded my fingers behind my head and listened, admiring the cloudless, starry sky. Beck was pretty damn good.

Just as my mind cleared of worry and the anxiety wafted away on Beck's smooth strings, footsteps shuffled behind me, bringing me back to reality. I turned my head to find Joan, my ex-assistant and Beck's girlfriend, walking toward me.

"I didn't know you were here this weekend," I said, a little more than surprised to see her. I did my very best to avoid any time alone with her, even though I knew Rachael was secure in our relationship. I didn't need to give her any reminders of our rocky beginning when she perceived my past romantic relationship with Joan as a threat.

"I got in late tonight by boat." Her eyes were lost in the trees, summoned by Beck's strings. "He's good," she said, stopping beside my chair.

"Exceptional."

The two of us listened silently until the melody ended. Then Joan turned to me. "You know he's wasting his talent being here."

My shoulders tensed. "Why do I hear accusation in your tone?" I had never had an indication that Beck wanted to do something other than work as crew foreman for Rocha Enterprises. I wasn't holding him hostage. Beck was a grown man. He could do whatever he wanted with his life. His choice. He certainly didn't need another man telling him what he should be doing.

"He feels obligated to you. He doesn't want to leave you high and dry here."

I scratched my chin, running my short nails through the stubble. "This project is over. Has been. Why does he feel he needs to stay?"

"Now that you sold off all of your properties, making Rocha Enterprises all but extinct, and you and he have become good friends..." She shrugged.

"It's his way of being supportive or something? Showing loyalty?" Jesus, I didn't sell all my properties by choice—my bastard father would've taken them from me if I hadn't. There was no way I'd let my hard work fall into those conniving hands. The last thing I wanted was to be an obligation, like someone's decrepit old grandparent. "He doesn't owe me anything."

"It's not about owing you. It's about standing by someone he thinks of like a brother. With everything going on—losing the company, MJ, Nadia—he won't leave Turtle Tear. And now there's the Weston Plantation. MJ will need him as foreman there." She shot me a challenging look, lifting a brow, and I knew what she was saying. What she was asking.

I nodded and turned away, trying to block out thoughts of the conversation I'd have to have. She stood for a moment longer before padding to the gate and heading off toward the boathouse in a golf cart.

I stretched my arms over my head before standing and inhaling a deep breath of lime-scented air. It was late fall, and Mr. Simcoe and I had cleaned up the overripe key limes from the orchard floor, but their sweet, pungent scent still lingered in the earth below the trees.

From now until the day I died, this would always be what I identified as the scent of home. This island, this hotel, Rachael. The awareness of home was something I'd never known before. Experiencing it gave me a heady feeling as I blew out a breath and turned toward the patio doors to find Rachael lingering in the entryway watching me. Her hair hung down past her shoulders to touch the lace trim on the top of her silky tank. Her matching pajama shorts clung to every curve. She was a sexy angel standing there beckoning me to her.

"Come back to bed," she said, holding her hand out. "Let me help you get your mind off things."

I took her hand and kissed it. She radiated sexual heat and emotional warmth. Two things I could never live without. Only from her. My Rachael.

My home.

It wasn't the first night I'd been stricken by the thought, tying her in with my base needs and desires. Over the months we'd been together, it was clear that I never wanted to be without her. I had to make sure she knew, she felt the same.

Soon. I'd do it soon.

I trailed my eyes from hers, down over her lips, neck, and to the spot on her collarbone where I knew I could make her sigh by kissing it.

Very soon.

Two

Rachael

"Your hands should be illegal," I whispered between moans of ecstasy. I grasped his wrist and tried to pull his hand away. I'd already had two orgasms and he was showing no sign of relenting. "I'm supposed to be taking *your* mind off of things."

Merrick chuckled against my breast and flicked his tongue across my nipple. "You have taken my mind off of things, just not these things." He sucked my stiffened peak and delved his fingers inside me deeper. My eyes rolled up to the ceiling, recalling a time when I wouldn't let him touch me.

Never again. I wanted his hands, his fingers, his mouth on me until my last breath. I'd given myself over to him and never once looked back. He was my life. Existing without him would be no existence at all.

The telltale quaking of my legs paired with the heat igniting in my center told me I was on the brink of my third mind-blowing climax of the night. "Please," I whimpered. "Merrick—I need..." I pulled on his shoulders, desperate to have him inside me. "Please."

He kissed his way up my chest to my neck, allowing me

to wrap my legs around his waist. "You never have to beg me, Rach, but I like it when you do."

I arched my back, loving the sensation of my sensitive nipples rubbing against his chest, and reached between us to wrap my hand around his long, hard penis. He groaned and I took his mouth with mine, sucking his lips and sliding my tongue against his.

I guided him to my opening. He barely thrust, entering me only an inch or so. I raised my hips, eager to take more of him in. "Slow," he whispered, threading his fingers with mine and raising them above my head. "Let me make love to you slowly."

I slid my legs down his, wrapping my ankles around his calves, feeling the length of his body pressed against mine, hot and heavy.

He rocked into me, pushing himself in a little at a time. The sensation—the waiting—was overwhelming. It brought tears to my eyes. I loved him so much, sometimes I couldn't keep it all inside. I felt like I'd explode with it.

I rocked with him. He looked down into my eyes and I blinked back the tears. "Why are you crying?" He kissed my forehead and each eyelid.

"Happy tears," I said. "I love you so much it hurts."

Merrick lowered his head and kissed my chest over my heart. "You have my love forever. I promise you. You believe that, don't you?"

I nodded. Fat, wet tears slipped down the sides of my face onto the pillow. "I want forever."

"Good," he said, following the salty trail of my tears with his tongue, down below my ear. "Because you don't have a choice." He thrust hard and deep, making me gasp and squeeze his hands. I tightened around him, wanting to give back the sensation he was giving me. He let out a low groan and leaned his forehead against mine.

I stared into his eyes as I rose up to meet each of his torturously slow and controlled thrusts. He ground his hips against mine, rubbing and circling his pelvis, hitting all the right spots inside and out. I whimpered and closed my eyes, knowing I wasn't going to last long. Merrick nuzzled my nose with his. "Open," he whispered. "I want to be looking in your eyes when I take you over the edge."

I did what he asked, locked in to his deep, dark, endless eyes. A rush of heat flushed my body. I tried to free my hands, wanting to grip his hair, pull him closer, but he wouldn't let go, only held my hands captive above me even tighter. "Come with me," I pleaded. "It's so close. Merrick..."

A tightening pulled behind my navel, spread through me, contracting around him.

"God, Rachael," he whispered.

I felt him throb inside me and I shattered with him.

Both breathless and sated, he collapsed on top of me for a moment, capturing my lips in a lingering kiss before rolling off and wrapping his arms around me, pulling me into him. "I love you. You're everything to me."

My heart jolted and swelled. I kissed his chest, savoring

the salty flavor of sweat, and nestled down into his arms. "I love you, too. No matter what."

He glanced down at me; his serious expression took my breath away. "Promise me," he said.

"I promise you. Forever."

He traced his finger over my eyebrows, down my nose, and across my lips. "I'm going to hold you to that."

"Promises should be sealed with a kiss." I kissed his fingertips, then lifted my head to reach his neck, his soft stubbled chin, and finally his lips, which I could never imagine getting enough of.

Three

Merrick

I woke with a start, blurry-eyed, to the shrill ringtone of my cell phone on the nightstand. I glanced at the clock. Three a.m. Who the hell was calling at this hour?

Rachael mumbled in her sleep and rolled over. Sometimes, I swore a bomb could go off and she wouldn't wake. I chalked it up to being overly worn out from our earlier activities.

Grabbing my phone, I answered it quickly, not recognizing the number, eager to silence the ear-numbing ring. "Hello?"

There was a moment of silence before a tentative female voice said, "It's Nadia."

"Where are you?" I asked, instantly awake and alert.

"Paris. I'm sorry."

I sat up, throwing my legs over the side of the bed and rubbing my eyes with my free hand. "Where in Paris?"

Because she'd come into my life under the influence of my father's betrayal, I didn't want to care about her, but Jesus, she was my flesh and blood, just like MJ. I had to care. I couldn't make myself *not* care.

I felt Rachael's hand on my back and looked over my shoulder at her. *Nadia*, I mouthed. Her eyes went wide.

"Rue Lincoln in the Golden Triangle. I can't talk, they're waking up. I'll call tomorrow," Nadia said and hung up.

I let my hand drop, holding my phone in my lap. "Paris." I blew out a hard breath and turned to face Rachael. "She said, 'They're waking up.' She's with Enzo and her mom. We're going to Paris. I'm bringing her back."

Rachael sat up. "We're going to Paris? Why?"

Her eyes were sleepy and her hair tangled in the back. I reached up and smoothed it down.

How could I explain why I had to go to Nadia in a way that would make sense when Nadia had come to us—to Turtle Tear—so underhandedly, working for my father. She'd been motivated to reveal herself as my daughter by his promises and then found out that Enzo Rocha wasn't a man who kept his promises.

Nadia *was* my daughter, though, and I couldn't believe she'd hurt me without the coercion of her grandfather and her mother, whom I'd believed had died during childbirth twenty years ago.

"I know," I said. "The situation is crazy, but I can't let her stay with them."

"Merrick..." Rachael dropped her eyes to her lap. "You don't think this is just another one of Enzo's games?"

"No. I heard desperation in Nadia's voice. She doesn't want to be there with them."

Rachael looked up at me from under her lashes. "She's helped him before. That's all I'm saying."

I clenched the sheet, willing myself to stay calm. Rachael had her reasons for wanting me to stay away from Nadia, but she had to understand why I couldn't. The girl was my daughter. "You don't trust her?" I knew she didn't, so it came out as a statement more than a question.

"No."

My back stiffened, but I wouldn't let this come between us. I'd figure out how to make Rachael see that this time with Nadia was different. "Then trust me."

She pressed her lips together and nodded. "Always."

I glanced toward the hotel. Still no sign of Rachael. She'd run back inside to grab something she'd forgotten and it was taking her forever to come back out. I was trying not to get impatient as Beck stowed our luggage in the helicopter and got it ready for takeoff.

It was time to have the conversation with him I'd been dreading. I wanted everything off my plate before leaving for Paris so I could concentrate completely on getting Nadia away from my father.

"I need to talk to you," I said to him, taking another glance toward the hotel. Still no Rachael. I gave Joan a sly nod.

"That doesn't sound good," Beck said, laughing it off. "I didn't do it."

I gestured for Beck to follow me a few yards away by

the tree line, then turned to face my best friend. "What are you doing here?"

Beck's forehead creased. "What are you talking about?"

"The project's done. Rocha Enterprises is gone. What are you doing here?" The only way around this situation was to plow straight through it. Not allowing Beck time to respond, I crossed my arms and continued. "You're a cellist, not a foreman. That's where you came from and where you need to go back to."

Beck ran a hand over his head and back along the ponytail at the base of his neck. "I'm not a cellist and I can't leave—"

"You can. You will, and you are a cellist. You used to play in an orchestra back in Nebraska, right? Isn't that what you told me when I interviewed you? I have no clue why you stopped playing and I'd love to hear the story someday, but there's no time right now. I'm leaving and so are you. I don't want you here when I get back."

At Beck's narrowed eyes and fists coming up to his hips, I swallowed hard, knowing Rachael would be back any second and I couldn't back down now. "Beck, you're fired. I no longer require a foreman. Go back to Nebraska and take that cello with you."

Beck spit on the ground. "You're a fucking bastard."

I took a step forward. "A fucking bastard who knows when a friend needs to hear the hard truth. Whatever you're afraid of in your past needs to be dealt with. You have serious talent. Don't waste it."

Beck shook his head. "You don't know what you're talking about."

"No? Go back there, get your ass back in that orchestra, and prove me wrong." I gritted my teeth. I didn't want Beck to leave, but it was time for him to find his own life and not get waylaid at Turtle Tear, bogged down with my issues.

"Whatever." Beck reached out and punched my shoulder. "Get the fuck out of here and find your daughter."

I knew my words hurt him, but also knew they struck a chord. I hoped this wouldn't create a rift between us any more than the distance between Florida and Nebraska would.

Rachael finally arrived with the whine of a golf cart, parked it, and hopped out. Joan gave me a tight-lipped smile and I gave one back. "Take care of him," I told her.

"If he'll let me," she said, gazing past me to the tree line, where Beck still stood with his arms folded, lost in thought.

I took a tote bag from Rachael. "You finally ready?" I twirled a lock of her hair that had fallen from the messy bun she'd wound up on top of her head. I liked it when she wore her hair like that and I could see the graceful lines of her neck.

"Ready." She waved to Beck, exchanged a handshake with Joan that wasn't unfriendly—the secrets of the Weston Plantation had created some strange bond between the two of them—and hooked her arm through mine. "Fly me to Paris, my love."

Four

Rachael

After a three-hour flight from Miami to New York, a two-hour layover, and a seven-hour overnight flight to Paris, we finally made it to Hotel Montalembert at 7 a.m. the next day. I was exhausted and never wanted to fly again. I was contemplating what I could do to convince Merrick to buy an apartment there and never leave just to avoid airports and the crimp in my neck that trying to sleep on a plane gave me.

Once in our room, I crashed onto the bed and announced, "I'm starving!"

"Twenty-four-hour room service," Merrick said, sitting on the side of the bed and opening the menu. "What would you like?"

"Anything. I'm going to spend some time in the bathroom making myself feel human again." I got up and pranced into the bathroom, blowing him a kiss before closing the door.

Then I sank back against it and closed my eyes. I was trying my best to keep a brave face for him, to not let any of this get to me. He was suffering enough as it was without my emotions piling on and causing him to worry. But Enzo Rocha was an entity all his own, and I didn't know what to expect from him. He'd proved through his lies, manipulation, and most recently, physical assault, that he was capable of anything at all. And he hated Merrick.

I'd never been so afraid in my life, even waking up tied to a bed in a strange hotel with a man I didn't realize I knew—yes, Merrick and I had come far. More than far. It seemed we'd spanned lifetimes in the space of several months together. I trusted and loved him absolutely. If this thing with Enzo went badly...

I couldn't even bring myself to think about it. I was probably being overdramatic.

Splashing water on my face, I prayed silently that we would get Nadia and return quickly to Turtle Tear. Until we did, our future seemed like a very distant place. This new transition in Merrick's life needed to end before we could find our peace and happiness together.

I took my hair down and brushed it, got rid of my blouse and pants, and squared my shoulders before walking back out into the room and facing Merrick. I'd be strong for him.

Sitting on the edge of the bed, he looked me over from head to toe and smirked. "You know I want to take that bra and those panties off of you and make you scream my name, but right now I'm so tired I can't even think straight."

I stepped between his knees and kissed the tip of his nose. "I'm just changing into something more comfortable.

No pressure tonight—today—whenever it is. I've lost all track of time."

"Me, too." He glanced at his cell phone lying on the bed beside him.

"Still nothing from her?" Nadia hadn't contacted Merrick again, and I knew it was making him crazy to be this close and have no contact.

"No. Nothing." He scratched his head and lay back against the plush pillows.

"How long are you going to wait before you call her?"

"Can't." He sighed. "It's a new number. If I know it, it'll tip Enzo off that she's contacted me, and it seemed like she wanted to keep that a secret."

I sat down beside him and ran my hand up his stomach over his chest. "So we wait?"

"We wait." He closed his eyes and I stroked his hair. Some things were worth waiting for.

There would be a day when this was all behind us. I just hoped I didn't have to wait too long for that day to arrive. Merrick would stop at no length to make up the lost time between him and his kids, but I didn't understand why Nadia, at almost twenty-one, couldn't just leave her grandfather and find her way to Turtle Tear. What was she afraid of? Or was it something else? Did she know something that Enzo was keeping under wraps, so he was keeping her close?

Several minutes later, the knock on the door from room service came as I lounged on the balcony taking in the view of the Eiffel Tower and the back of Notre Dame while Merrick showered. He stepped out of the bathroom clad in pajama bottoms as I opened the door and the waiter rolled our order in on a cart.

"Thank you," Merrick said, tipping the man while I took inventory of the tray. "Fruit, a baguette, cheese, wine."

"I didn't order wine." Merrick strode over and picked up the bottle. A tag hung from the neck by a string. He picked it up and read it, frowning. "Welcome to Paris." He glanced at the waiter. "Is this complimentary?"

"*Non, monsieur.* It was added to your room service order."

"By who?" He set the bottle down, lines forming across his forehead.

"Je ne sais pas, monsieur."

Merrick nodded, accepting the waiter's answer that he didn't know who'd sent the wine. "Thank you. That's all we'll be needing right now."

"Bien."

Merrick closed and locked the door. I lifted the tag and read the slanted, masculine writing. "What do you think?" I asked.

Merrick shook his head. "I don't know."

"Enzo? Nadia?"

"Could be anyone. Could be MJ or Beck and Joan, for all we know." He gazed at me and shrugged.

I knew he didn't believe that. "It says, 'Welcome to Paris.' That implies whoever sent it is already here, welcoming us."

"There's no way to know who it came from. Let's just eat and get some rest." He pulled a chair out for me at the round glass table.

I sat and plucked a ripe strawberry from one of the dishes on the tray. My stomach hurt so badly, even though I was starving, I had no appetite. Damn Enzo Rocha. I knew that bottle of wine was from him.

Although exhausted, I didn't sleep. While Merrick napped, I got online and looked up as many apartments on Rue Lincoln that rented weekly as I could find. I called the phone numbers listed on the rentals, pretending to be Enzo's daughter in-law, hoping to find Nadia, but wasn't having any luck.

I was so focused on my search, I didn't hear Merrick come up behind me. "You'll never find them," he whispered in my ear, making me jump and grasp the arms of the chair.

"God, you scared me."

He swept my hair to the side and kissed my neck. "If Enzo doesn't want to be found, he won't be."

I closed my laptop. "Then why are we here?"

He traced my earlobe with the tip of his nose. "Nadia will contact me. She'll tell us where to find her."

I wanted to believe that. I heard the desperation in his voice. He didn't want to believe his daughter would betray him and be loyal to Enzo. I hoped for his sake—for all of their sakes—Nadia would get in touch.

Merrick took my hands and pulled me up out of my chair, wrapping his arms around me and holding me against him. "Let's get out of here and go look around."

He kissed me. I remembered our first kiss and how I'd been so hesitant, so nervous, but my raw lust for Merrick took over and I couldn't hold myself back. Now my lust and desire pooled with comfort and love. His kisses made me feel cherished and treasured as well as physically wanted.

It was so clear to me, even though neither one of us had actually spoken the word *marriage*, that he was my husband. He would be—it was meant to be. I felt the white, hot truth of it in every cell of my body. We were one soul, torn in half and put on earth to find each other.

And there he was, right in front of me. He'd made it happen. He must've somehow known deep inside that I belonged with him.

"Why are you staring at me like that?" he asked, a cocky grin forming on his lips.

I rose up on my toes to kiss him again. "Like what?"

"Like you have some dangerous secret." He pinned my hands behind my back and pressed me into the wall. "Are you keeping something from me, Ms. DeSalvo?"

"Nothing you don't already know," I said, smiling.

"And what's that?" He nuzzled my neck. It tickled and I leaned my head against his, laughing.

"You'll figure it out sooner or later," I said, nipping his earlobe. "I'm just giving you time."

Merrick chuckled and rested his forehead against mine. "Is that so? How much time do you think I need?"

I shrugged playfully, wondering if he knew what I was referring to.

"Maybe you're the one who needs time." He winked.

Caught off guard, my pulse quickened. Were we talking about the same thing? Marriage? Why was he giving *me* time? I was waiting on *him*. "Maybe I don't."

He stepped back and turned me toward the big suitcase, still packed and sitting beside the bed. "Maybe you should change out of that robe and get dressed so we can get out of here." He smacked me on the bottom to get me moving.

Padding across the plush carpet, I felt my heart sink a little at his dismissal of the conversation we'd been circling so closely. His giving me time sounded like a poor excuse.

I knelt on the floor and began to dig through the clothes I'd brought.

I was so certain we were on the same page, just not verbalizing it yet. But…maybe we weren't on the same page?

Five

Merrick

Rachael was quiet. Something was wrong. Only a half an hour earlier, we were joking and laughing, tiptoeing around discussing the Big M—marriage. I didn't want to avoid it any longer. I was never one for treading lightly around anything—just the opposite. My reputation for charging into things like a rodeo bull preceded me. But she wasn't ready for a proposal. No matter how perfect we were together, and no matter how confident I was that we'd end up at the end of that aisle someday soon, Rachael wasn't ready to say yes to me down on one knee with a ring.

This wasn't something I'd bully her into. I'd wait. If I'd learned one thing from our relationship, it was that putting my impulsiveness under wraps until the time was right to act was key. But walking beside me, back stiff, shoulders straight, doing her best to look anywhere but at me, she was clearly pissed.

I squeezed her hand. "What's wrong?"

"Nothing." She didn't bother looking at me.

"Rachael, we're in the most romantic city on earth, walking down the street. There's the Eiffel Tower." I pointed at the enormous structure only a block or so away. "There are cafés and boutiques on every corner. Look." I gestured to a table-lined sidewalk across the street. "We can stop for a glass of wine if you'd like."

She did look at me then and gave me a smile, but it was anything but heartfelt. "No thanks. I'm fine."

I flipped through my internal catalog of what to do when Rachael was mad. Admittedly, it wasn't a very foolproof catalog. Typically, it got me into more trouble. "Since this is your first time here, we should go through the Louvre." Being a designer and an architect, she'd love it, I was sure.

She shrugged. "Maybe tomorrow."

Now she was just being stubborn. "Okay. I'll leave the plan up to you. I'm enjoying being here in your company."

"Let's just walk," she said.

So we kept on, down the bustling sidewalk full of Parisians and tourists alike. As she stalked down the Champs-Élysées, her foul mood kept her from taking in her surroundings. She hadn't even commented on the Arc de Triomphe. This couldn't stand. "Rachael, I—"

"Let's go in here," she said, cutting me off and pushing open the door of a jewelry store. I followed, grateful for her showing interest in anything. Hell, I'd buy her ten-thousand-dollar earrings if it would make her happy.

But I soon realized it wasn't earrings she was after. She stopped directly in front of the case holding diamond rings—engagement rings to be precise—and I was screwed.

"Can I help you?" a woman asked in a Parisian accent. Her hair was pulled back severely from her face and secured in a tight bun behind her head. Her slim, long tailored skirt and jacket made me think of an evil stepmother from some kids' movie I saw on HBO. Nanny McSomething or other. Her drawn expression did little to make me eager to spend money in the store.

"These are all so lovely," Rachael said, admiring the rings. "Don't you think so, Merrick?"

My throat constricted and I swallowed hard, trying to stay in control. My mind practically itched to be spontaneous and go along with her. We could be married by nightfall. She looped her arm through mine and there was no escape. "Yes. Lovely," I said, almost choking on the words.

"You're right. This is the most romantic place on earth." She sighed longingly.

The situation was so contrived—so unlike Rachael—I stifled a laugh that would get me a murderous glare and the silent treatment for at least a week. She couldn't be more obvious about her intentions, but she still hadn't just tried talking to me about it.

"Would you like me to take one out for you?" the saleswoman asked, darting glances between me and Rachael.

"No," I said, and felt Rachael stiffen beside me. She dropped her arm from mine. "We're just looking today. Thank you."

I wouldn't be bullied into this either, not to mention the fact that I already had the ring and it was sitting in my suitcase back at the hotel. I'd been carrying it around with me fighting the urge to drop down in front of her and beg her never to leave me.

It just seemed so fast. She needed more time. I knew she did, even if she couldn't admit it to herself.

I leaned in and whispered in her ear, "Now's not the right time."

Her chest expanded with air and she held it in. I was afraid she was gearing up to let me have it. But she slowly let out her breath. "Thank you," she said to the woman with a curt nod before pivoting and heading for the door without one glance in my direction.

I followed her out, grabbing the door before it shut in my face. "Rachael?" I called, catching up with her.

"Just don't. There's nothing to say." She rounded on me, jutting out a hip. "Unless you want me to go back home to my mother again since I'm being unreasonable?"

Of course she'd throw the last time we'd had...differences of opinion, up in my face. "No. I thought we were past that. I was stupid. I don't want you to go anywhere. Ever." I reached for her hand and she turned away.

"Yeah, you've proven that."

Jesus. This woman would be the death of me yet. "Rachael. Do you honestly think I don't want to be with you?"

She let out a sharp laugh, her hair bouncing up and down with each hard step away from me. "I'm beginning to." The words were thrown carelessly over her shoulder.

My temper simmered. One more comment like that and it would flare out of control. I put a hand out and caught her by the shoulder, firmly stopping her in her tracks. "Don't."

She stopped and let me step up beside her, crossing her arms over her chest. She turned her head away, furiously wiping her fingers under her eyes.

Guilt and regret swept through me. I'd failed her. Again. "You're crying."

"I'm humiliated," she snapped.

"Humiliated?" I dropped my head, shaking it. Hurting her was the worst feeling in the world. I hated myself every single time I fucked up. "I'll go back in there right now and buy you a ring. Five rings. Hell, the whole freaking case if that's what you want."

Rachael turned her eyes on me and I flinched. I'd never seen her so . . . raw with anger. "This isn't about what *I* want."

I steadied myself, trying not to let my emotions reflect hers. One of us had to stay calm and rational. I ran my hands up her arms. "I—" My phone rang, sparking every nerve in my body. I grabbed it from my pocket. It was the number I'd been waiting for. "It's her. Nadia."

Six

Rachael

I willed myself to let my embarrassment slide away as Merrick answered his phone. I'd been foolish to think he'd take the bait dangled in front of his nose in the jewelry store. Soon, though, I'd have to find out one way or the other. I wanted this man for life, and if he was just planning on riding our relationship out for years without making it official...well, I wouldn't let that happen. I wanted a husband. Kids. A family of our own. Yes, we had time, but if he wasn't feeling what I was feeling...If his idea of a future wasn't on track with what I had in mind...

"Fine," he said into the phone, eyeing me like he was trying to read my mind while listening to Nadia.

I glanced down to my feet. It could wait. My main concern was getting this nightmare over with. Then we could move on with our lives—come what may.

Or may not.

He hung up. "They've moved locations."

My head snapped up. "The wine was from him, wasn't it?"

He nodded slowly. His jaw clenched and brow knit with anger.

"Why doesn't she just leave? Does she even want to?"

His expression turned stern. "She'll call when she can."

I bit my lip, wanting to ask if he could trust Nadia, or if she was leading us on some crazy chase through France. Speaking for myself, I wouldn't put one ounce of faith in the girl.

"What now?" I asked.

"Now?" Merrick turned his head from side to side, taking in our surroundings. "We enjoy fall in Paris." He caught my eyes and cocked a brow. "Unless you'd rather argue some more and doubt my love for you?" His hands came up and cupped my face. "Trust me, Rachael. Have faith in what I feel for you, what I want for us."

I held his warm, dark eyes as his lips came closer to mine, felt his breath on my cheek, and let go of my anxiety. His kiss eased my mind and filled me with certainty. It would happen for us, and just like his slow, languorous kiss, there was no reason to rush it.

Evening found us strolling along the Seine, hand in hand. We'd done some shopping at the high-end stores and leisured over an early-afternoon bottle of wine at an outdoor café. Content and still jet-lagged, I enjoyed the sun slanting on the water, warming my shoulders as we neared the Eiffel Tower.

I couldn't believe I was here. There hadn't been time to think about it, or plan for it; we just left Turtle Tear and here we were. Sometimes life with Merrick Rocha was jarring. I glanced at him out of the corner of my eye and felt one side of my mouth rise in a slight smile. He'd never be predictable, that was for sure. My life would never be boring. If our life together charted down the same course it had been on, there was no way to determine where we would end up.

"River dinner cruise?" he asked, nodding toward a launch pier at the foot of the Eiffel Tower where tourists were purchasing tickets and boarding a long boat with a large deck on the front and down the sides. The center was framed with windows for sightseeing. "I don't know about you, but sitting back on a boat, relaxing and taking in the monuments, sounds like a great idea to me."

I reached up and stroked his cheek. I hadn't known I was going to touch him; sometimes my body worked on autopilot when I was close to him. "Sounds perfect."

We made our way onto the front deck of the boat and stood at the railing looking out at Paris from the water. It was a design architect's dream. "Did you know," I asked, grabbing Merrick's arm, "that the Eiffel Tower was built as a temporary exhibit for the World's Fair in 1889?"

His eyes flashed as he smiled. "No. I didn't know that."

I knew he had to have known. There was no way he didn't, but I loved that he didn't want to quench my excitement. I narrowed my eyes at him and grinned back.

"What?" He chuckled.

"Nothing."

"Tell me more about the city's architecture," he said, waving a hand toward the wide avenues and masses of buildings.

"Well, in the mid-1800s, the city went through a massive remodeling, and for the most part, it's what we see today. The second empire building codes are still in place if you can believe that." I felt a little lighter talking about my favorite subject. Architecture was a language in which I was more than fluent.

Merrick became very serious, studying my face closely.

"What?" I asked. His expression was suddenly so odd.

He shook his head, coming out of whatever thought process had taken over his mind. "I like hearing you talk about what you're passionate about."

I nudged him with my hip. "I wasn't talking about you."

"I know." He wrapped an arm around my waist and pulled me close. "It seems like so many times women lose themselves when they're in a relationship. I'm glad you're still you. I don't want Turtle Tear—or me—to define you. Even though Rocha is no longer in the development business, I hope you'll take on other projects. I can help you make connections with some of my contacts. You just say the word."

And just when I thought I couldn't fall more in love with him. Is this what all of his hesitation was about? He didn't want me forgetting myself and who I was? I turned into him, pressing against his chest as I hugged him. "I'm not ready yet, but when I am, I'll let you know. And Merrick"—I let him go enough to look into his eyes—"losing myself to you wouldn't be such a terrible thing. If I ever did, it would be by choice, not by weakness."

He laughed as the breeze off the water blew through his hair. "I don't think you've got a weak bone in your body, Ms. DeSalvo. You're one stubborn woman who knows how to get what she wants."

"I never used to be, Mr. Rocha. I blame you for that."

"That's something I don't mind taking credit for." He kissed me and the boat lurched under our feet. A horn blew above the wheelhouse, signaling our departure from the pier.

Dinner was served inside the glass-encased boat at a window-side, white-clothed table as we cruised past the Musée d'Orsay, Notre Dame, and La Conciergerie. We dined on salmon and braised fennel, chilled courgette cream soup, and mixed Riviera salads. Stuffed, we picked at our desserts, cherry clafoutis with almond cream, and sipped chardonnay. I detected distress hidden in Merrick's eyes over his wineglass. He was not a patient man, and not being able to locate Nadia was eating away at him.

I reached across the table and took his hand. "The sun's setting. Let's go back out onto the deck and watch."

The pink-and-orange-streaked sky blazing behind the Louvre took my breath away and made my knees weak. "Can you believe how beautiful..." I could only shake my head in disbelief.

Out of the corner of my eye, I caught Merrick focusing his phone on me for a photo as I leaned over the railing, staring into the sky reflected in the water beneath us. "I've never seen anything more astoundingly gorgeous in my life," he said, snapping the picture as I turned to look at him.

"This has been the best afternoon." I smiled, thinking back to all of our afternoons together. "Not the best ever, but close."

Merrick stood behind me and wrapped his arms around me, leaning his chin on my shoulder. "Not the best ever? Which was the best ever?"

Heat gathered between my legs as he flattened his palms against my stomach and ran his hands down to the tops of my thighs and up over my hips, pulling me back against him and discreetly grinding himself into me.

I let my head fall back against his shoulder and stared up at the swirling, blinding colors in the sky. "There was this afternoon in a tree house with chocolate-raspberry cake that comes to mind."

"Mmm," he groaned in my ear, "the *first* afternoon. I agree, that was a good one, but..."

He pressed himself against me again, holding me so tight, I could barely breathe. "But?" I whispered.

"No matter how much I agree that afternoon was pretty spectacular, the one that stands out in my mind is a certain time we walked in on our friends and then I took you against the door of our bedroom."

Oh God, that memory made me dizzy with lust. "How

much longer is this cruise?" I heard the desperation in my voice. "And how far is our hotel?"

Merrick chuckled, a deep, guttural sound in my ear that made my spine tingle. "Who says you need to wait?" His hand slipped inside my jacket between the wide-set buttons. His fingers slid down inside my pants, underneath my lace-trimmed underwear.

"Merrick," I whispered, unable to tell him to stop, but mortified at what we were doing in public.

"Shh...enjoy the view while I enjoy you." He nodded toward the bank. "Look, there's Le Grand Palais." He nuzzled his nose into my neck and breathed me in as his deft fingers alternated between working inside me and rubbing my cleft in small, tantalizing circles. "I remember the first time I saw you touching yourself like this. I thought I would die of wanting you that night."

I rocked slightly against his hand, not enough to make anyone take notice of what we were doing. "I wanted you, too. Why do you think I was touching myself?" I smiled, then inhaled sharply as he pressed a second finger inside me.

"We're coming up on La Statue de la Liberté. We'll be reaching the pier soon." He lightly bit my neck and rubbed me faster, harder, rolling his fingers up and down while they circled.

I thought I might die of embarrassment, because there was no way to stifle my breathless gasps of pleasure.

I grasped his hand through my pants and held on as he brought me to the edge and then past with thrusts of his fingers inside me. I squeezed his forefinger tight, feeling myself throb and pulse around him while he held me up against the railing.

"That's it," he whispered, kissing my temple. "The perfect evening."

He slipped his hand free and spun me to face him. Gathering my hair back from my face, he held my head in his hands and kissed me. His warm, wonderful lips conveyed more than any words ever could.

The sound of the boat horn startled us apart. "Back at the pier," I said, brushing another kiss on his mouth.

"Just in time." He winked and gave me a sultry grin.

"You'll get yours later," I said, wondering where I could stop and surprise him on our way back to the hotel.

Seven

Merrick

The streets were alive with lights and music, a fall festival with street vendors and carnival rides. I watched the way the flashes of color caught Rachael's eyes. A pack of little kids ran toward us, chasing and laughing, dodging us at the last moment, but catching Rachael's bag with a sticky red candy apple.

"Be careful!" I shouted after them.

"It's okay," Rachael said, digging a tissue from her bag and wiping the mess off the best she could.

"One of them is going to end up hurt," I said, watching the retreating kids.

"Paternal instinct kicking in?" Rachael quirked a smile.

I stuffed my hands in my pockets. "Better late than never, I suppose." Her eyes fell and her hands fumbled with the tissue, crumpling it before tucking it back inside her bag. It struck me that maybe she'd mentioned my paternal instinct as a way to open the conversation about our future. Would we have kids someday? Rachael was only in her twenties; surely she'd want to have kids.

Maddie and MJ would get married and have kids. Jesus,

I could be a grandfather before I was a father again. Or at the same time. This wasn't supposed to happen in a man's early thirties.

I was just getting used to the idea of being a father to MJ. I was trying my best to deal with Nadia. I wasn't ready to think about a future kid, but my mind was flashing images of Rachael holding an infant in our bed in the tree house with the wispy bed curtains blowing around them in the breeze from the open windows.

It was a nice image. A perfect image. I wanted it—wanted to see it with my eyes and not just my imagination.

I'd get to be there this time from conception until the day I died. I'd never let what happened with MJ and Nadia happen between me and Rachael's child.

I took her hand in both of mine and held it against my chest. She gazed up at me and I wanted to speak every word, every thought that I'd been thinking, but I couldn't bring myself to get them off of my tongue. What if I said something to scare her? I constantly made the wrong choices. Admittedly, I was terrible at communicating. It was our biggest obstacle. It was up to me to change it, though.

She blinked a few times, tilting her head and staring into my eyes, like she was trying to decipher what was going on in my head. "You can tell me," she said.

"I know. It's—you know me. I mess things up all the time. I need to think before I speak. It has to be said just right. I can't ruin it when it comes out of my mouth this time." I thought she knew what I was referring to, but to be certain, I rubbed my thumb in circles over her left ring finger. "I can't mess this up."

"You won't." Rachael leaned into me, wrapping her arms around my waist and resting her head against my chest. "Even if it doesn't come out perfectly, I know your heart, Merrick Rocha. That's what matters."

God, her words were a safety net. My apprehension of failing her melted away somewhat. "You *own* my heart, Rachael DeSalvo."

We strolled, hand in hand, through the carnival. I hadn't realized how far we'd walked that evening. The jet-lagged exhaustion I'd suffered earlier waned, tampered by the night air and excitement around us.

"What if she stays with Enzo?" Rachael said out of the blue. "Nadia. What then? Will it consume you for the rest of your life, or can you let it go?"

I shook my head. "Not an option. I got MJ away from him. I'll get Nadia, too."

As soon as I'd learned of MJ's existence—a fact hidden from me, along with the knowledge of his twin, for twenty years—I had to get him away from Enzo. I knew from personal experience what living with that man for even a short amount of time could do. Nadia had been fortunate enough to have been raised by her mother. Of course, I wasn't sure how much better that situation had been. I needed time with Nadia to know her, to understand what she'd been told about me for all of those years, to come to terms with having her exist in the first place.

Rachael pressed her lips together, making the outer edges turn white. "So your life—our life—is on hold until everything is perfect with MJ and Nadia? You know there's no such thing as perfect."

"Why are you in such a hurry?" The words were out in a rush, spurred on by her doubt and the tone of her disbelief that this would end up how I wanted it to. The stunned look on her face was like I'd physically attacked her. Wide-eyed, she dropped her hand from mine. "Jesus," I said, running my hands through my hair. "Believe me, I want exactly what you want. But right now, MJ and Nadia come first. Are you asking me to turn my back on them?"

She took a step up to me and jabbed a finger into my chest. "No! I'm asking you to not let them become your *entire* life. There's still *you* and what you want and need."

A flame lit in my gut. She thought I was a fool for following Nadia to Paris. "I should just go home, huh? Fuck Nadia. Shove my head in the sand and forget this ever happened? Go back to the fairy tale of Turtle Tear and pretend?"

"Is that what you do there, Merrick? Pretend?" Her eyes blazed with anger and hurt. The same anger and hurt boiling over inside me.

"You can't seriously be asking me that. You think I pretend when I'm with you? Why the hell would I do that?"

Rachael turned away from me, took a deep breath, and blew it out hard. "It's been a long day. Let's just get back to the hotel."

"Fine."

I didn't try to take her hand as we walked back in silence. Was I being irrational? Hell, I didn't know. I'd always let my instincts guide me. They were telling me to protect the people I loved. How could that be wrong?

Back at the hotel, Rachael locked herself in the bathroom and took a shower. She must not have realized how thin the walls were, because I heard her sobbing.

I sat on the foot of the bed and stared at my reflection in the mirror over the dresser. "You know what she wants, you asshole. Give her the damn ring and make her happy."

Before I could argue with Mirror Me, I knelt beside my suitcase, unzipped the compartment in the bottom, and held the black velvet box in the palm of my hand.

The water shut off in the shower.

She'd be out any minute.

My eyes stayed glued to the ring box. Could I do this? Here? Now?

The bathroom doorknob turned.

I panicked and shoved the ring box back into the suitcase.

No. Not here. Not now. This was all wrong. We'd been fighting. She'd think the only reason I was proposing was because of our argument on the way back to the hotel. Plus, this wasn't the romantic spot I'd pictured.

"What are you looking for?" she asked, rubbing her wet hair with a towel.

"Um, making sure I brought my toothbrush." I grabbed my toothbrush and pulled it out, smiling.

She nodded, unaffected. "Bathroom's all yours."

Shit. She was emotionally drained. It was written all over her face in the circles under her puffy eyes and the red splotches on her cheeks. I should just give her the damn ring.

The entire time I showered, I debated with myself. I could order champagne and strawberries—no, brownie sundaes—from room service and snuggle up in bed with her and our dessert and give her the ring. But we'd had dessert on the boat.

I lathered soap on my chest and down over my stomach. The desperate feeling was making me crazy.

No, not tonight. I had to keep trusting my instincts. Tonight was not the night to ask Rachael to marry me.

Eight

Rachael

I woke up the next day sweating, with Merrick wrapped around me. He was like sleeping with a toaster oven. I'd fallen asleep while he was showering the night before and didn't even remember laying my head on the pillow.

In the streams of light filtering in through the filmy curtains, I ran my eyes up the strong arm wrapped around me. The bittersweet feeling broke my heart. I wanted to be held in his arms forever, but it seemed like it would never happen.

I knew it was early in our relationship to be thinking about forever and that it might not happen for us, but I knew his mind as well as his heart. If he needed to have the perfect world before he proposed, he never would. Perfect worlds don't exist. He'd never understand that.

So I either waited, or... Leaving him was unbearable to even consider.

Why was I doing this to myself? To us? Here we were in Paris, our relationship was in a wonderful place, and I was pushing and pushing him for more. Why?

If I really let myself examine my feelings, I could admit

I was afraid. I hadn't had enough time to be the most important person in his life, and now with MJ and Nadia, it seemed I'd always be second—third—best.

I turned my head and studied his face, his peaceful, sleeping face. He even looked strong and confident with his eyes closed, his long lashes splayed underneath them. My eyes traced his wide lips. I knew what they felt like on my own. His close beard felt prickly through my hair when he kissed the top of my head. I could feel the memory of it, and my scalp tingled. I'd explored his body, from his toes to the top of his head. Kissed, tasted, pleasured every inch.

He was mine. All I wanted was to keep him that way.

I leaned in and lightly kissed his lips, warm and soft. Always so warm and soft. I traced a finger over one eyebrow. He flinched, but didn't wake.

I rested my hand over his heart to feel it beating under my palm. There was no way I could ever love anyone as much as him.

Helpless—that was how I felt. The helplessness circled the fear, stalked around it, and poked it, making it raw and sore in my chest. I wanted to take the situation and resolve it quickly, but I couldn't.

Or could I?

My head snapped to the nightstand, where Merrick's cell phone was charging. I wouldn't let myself stop and ponder the consequences of what I was about to do.

Slipping out from under his arm and the heavy down comforter, I grabbed his phone off the nightstand. I stood frozen with it between my hands, watching him for signs of waking.

He sighed loudly and rolled over onto his stomach.

I dashed to the balcony, opened the door as quietly as I could, and stole away outside to make the call. The breeze was chilly through my short, lightweight nightgown, and chills climbed up my legs and over my bare bottom.

The number was the last on his incoming calls list. I peered over my shoulder through the glass door to Merrick sleeping in bed, knowing he'd be pissed when he found out I called.

I squeezed the phone in my hand. I couldn't let the helplessness win. I clicked the green send-call button and put the phone to my ear.

On the second ring, Nadia answered. "Dad, I told you, I'd call you. If he finds out I've been in contact with you, he'll destroy this phone and—"

"It's Rachael."

Neither of us said anything for a moment.

"Why are you calling?" Nadia asked.

"I want to help. I want this over. Where are you?"

"On a train in the south of France. I don't know where exactly. I was going to call when we got to wherever he's taking us."

"Who else is with you?"

"My mom."

Gina Montgomery, MJ and Nadia's mom, was with them. The woman who'd pretended she was dead for the past twenty years. The woman who let Enzo ruin Merrick's life. Money was a powerful motivator to keep secrets, and Enzo had given Gina a lot of it to keep her mouth closed. "Is she helping him, or does he have the two of you with him against your will?"

"She's with him. She's always been with him. I don't know…I've been confused. I'm trying to do what's right."

For a second, I felt sorry for Nadia. But only for a second. My distrust of Nadia kicked in and took over. "What train are you on? We'll be on the next one out of the station."

"I don't know, I—"

"Bullshit, Nadia! What train are you on? Either you want our help, or you're leading your dad on a wild-goose chase. Which is it?"

"Rachael." I snapped my head around at the sound of Merrick's voice. He stood in the doorway, seething.

I didn't care. This sit-and-wait business was killing us both. "Which is it, Nadia?" I continued, setting my eyes on Merrick's, daring him to make me stop.

He fisted his hands, and his jaw clenched along with every muscle in his bare chest and stomach. It wasn't the time for it, but I couldn't help admiring the beauty of a pissed-off Merrick, just awoken with his hair sexy and messed up, wearing nothing but pajama pants hanging low on his hips. The sight of him stirred my desire.

I knew how to calm him down when I was off the phone. I still owed him from the evening before anyway.

"I have to go," Nadia whispered. "Take the TGV out of Paris-Gare de Lyon to Nice-Ville." Then she hung up.

I lowered the phone from my ear. We stared at each other.

"Get what you wanted?" he asked, his tone dark and menacing.

"She said to take the train to Nice-Ville."

He shook his head. His impossibly dark eyes like granite pierced into mine.

"You're pissed," I said. "I knew you would be."

Hands on his hips, he took two steps toward me. "You did it anyway."

"Your judgment's clouded when it comes to Nadia." I sank onto the patio chair behind me, gripped the front of Merrick's pajama bottoms, and pulled him another step forward between my knees.

He glared down at me. "My judgment's clouded?"

"You want to trust her, so you do."

"So you take matters into your own hands?"

I leaned forward and grabbed the drawstring on his PJ bottoms with my teeth, pulling the bow free before hooking my thumbs into the waistband and tugging them down to drop at his ankles. Looking up at him, I ran my hands up his bare thighs and took his cock in my hands. "Yes. I'm taking matters into my own hands."

Merrick closed his eyes and took a deep breath, letting his head fall back slightly. "I'm so fucking pissed at you,

Rachael. I'm a man. I don't need you running interference. I can take whatever happens."

I licked him from base to tip, hearing the rush of air from his lungs. His hands came off his hips and threaded through my hair.

"So be fucking pissed. But you're mine. It's my job to take care of you." I took his rapidly growing length into my mouth. There was something so powerful about loving this man, about giving him pleasure and taking it from him. He was my addiction.

I pushed away the thought that we might be seen out on the balcony, too turned on by his arousal to care. The way he felt in my mouth—hot, silky, and huge—made me want to take him deeper, faster. My abandon of all reservations with Merrick was nothing I'd ever experienced before. I'd do anything to him, with him, and let him take me however he wanted.

Merrick fisted my hair in his hands and thrust himself in and out of my mouth. I knew he was working out his anger, but he'd stop if I wanted him to. I didn't. His frustration, eagerness, and lust fueled me. I reached between his legs, massaging his balls, working him into a panting frenzy. "Fuck, Rachael—killing me."

Merrick stepped back, pulling himself out of my mouth, holding the base of his cock, eyes flaming with heat and rage. He pulled me up and turned me around. "Bend over the chair."

My silky slip of a nightgown rose as I knelt on the

seat and leaned over the back. I closed my eyes as Merrick grasped both sides of my ass, slipping both thumbs between my cheeks and sliding them down to my middle, spreading my lips apart. I gripped the back of the chair tighter as he spread my wetness with his fingers, circling my clitoris before guiding the head of his cock to my opening and shoving his length inside in one fast, hard thrust.

I threw my head back, gasping and arching into him. So full. The sensation was always unexpected, no matter how many times he'd filled me.

He kept his grip on my ass cheeks as he slammed himself into me over and over, squeezing me so hard, I knew his fingertips would leave bruises, but the pinch of pain with the overwhelming pleasure thrilled me.

"Stay. Out. Of it," Merrick said, punctuating the words with deep thrusts. One hand grabbed a handful of my hair. "Am. I. Clear?" He pulled me back against him hard, using my hair like reins, to meet each brutal thrust. I cried out.

"Am. I. Clear?" he repeated, continuing his deep penetrating assaults.

"Yes!" I reached back and grabbed his thigh. My insides were quivering on the brink of my first pleasure/pain orgasm. "Please. Yes."

Merrick let go of my hair and wrapped his forearms around my waist, leaning over my back. "Let it go." His husky voice was like a growl in my ear.

I wasn't sure if he meant the situation with Nadia, or my own burgeoning release, but the blinding red heat behind my eyes and the prickling surge of energy sparking at every nerve ending were my answer.

I exploded, shattered, shook and convulsed, whimpered, and collapsed back against Merrick as a sob escaped my throat.

He collected me into his arms, lifted me from the chair, and carried me back to bed. The warmth of his chest against my cheek and his embrace cracked me open, and tears rolled from my eyes.

Merrick covered us with the down duvet and held me tight against him. "What is it? Was I too—"

"No," I whispered, placing a kiss over his heart. "It's just with everything—yesterday—the arguing, and you seem so far away, locked from me inside your head with this whole mess—I just..." I lifted my head, resting my chin on his chest to see his eyes, always so deep, their darkness so sincere. "I miss you."

Merrick traced a tear down my cheek, his finger featherlight on my skin. "I'm sorry. I want to be...I've never..." He trailed off, glancing up at the ceiling. "I want to be the kind father my own father never was. I can't screw this up."

Overwhelming feelings clenched in my chest, sending more tears flowing from my eyes. "Merrick," I said, my voice thick with emotion. I scooted up his body, resting on top of him. "I love you."

He held my head between his hands and kissed me. I tasted his sweet lips and my salty tears. His mouth moved over mine slowly, thoroughly. I cherished each and every kiss. Every touch. Every time we made love.

My fingers slid up the sides of his neck, the tips tickled by the hair on his nape. I treasured this man, could never imagine loving someone as much as I loved him. Never wanted to spend a day without him for the rest of my life.

Nine

Merrick

The train sped across the French countryside toward Nice. No matter how much I wanted to spend the next week locked in a Paris hotel room with Rachael, never getting dressed or leaving the bed, I couldn't abandon my fatherly duty to go to Nadia. She needed me.

I'd lost too much time with my kids already, and I'd make Enzo pay for every year. Every lie. Every pang of guilt over Gina Montgomery's death—fake death.

So many lies.

One mistake—sex with Gina—getting Gina pregnant when I was so young caused my father to set all of his devious plots against me into motion.

And God's honest truth: I couldn't even really remember sex with Gina Montgomery. It was all so awkward and over before it really began. More like a wet dream than a first time.

"What are you thinking about?" Rachael said, startling me from the thoughts running through my mind as fast as the train. I turned away from the window to face her. Her open expression, wide, eager eyes, and warm voice sucked me in every time.

I could never keep anything from her, even if I wanted to. She was a seductive force of nature, plying words off my tongue without me even realizing.

"I don't remember being with Gina."

Rachael's eyes flickered. "You don't?"

I shrugged. "It was a long time ago. I was way too young. I don't imagine it was all that memorable for her either." I chuckled, hoping to play it off. It bothered me, but it shouldn't. Why did it matter if I remembered? I got MJ out of the deal. And Nadia.

She watched me for a moment, curiosity written all over her face.

"What?"

She shook her head. "Nothing."

I almost prodded her to tell me what was on her mind, but let it go as she tucked back into the book she'd been reading. There was nothing left to say anyway. The past was the past.

I just wished my crazy-ass past would stop butting in between us. I wanted to give Rachael the life she deserved, not some dramatic emotional roller coaster. I reached over and rested my hand on her thigh, craving the contact that always calmed my racing mind and rattled nerves. She leaned her head against my shoulder and turned the page of her book, sighing contentedly.

We had another thirty minutes until we reached the Aix-en-Provence station and transferred trains. After that, it was another three hours to Nice. Rachael hadn't known which leg of the trip Nadia, Gina, and Enzo were on, or if they were already in Nice, or staying, or moving on.

It was like chasing shadows.

We arrived at the Nice-Ville station in late evening. The sun had set, but it wasn't yet dark. I wanted to think of this trip as a grand adventure, a trip of a lifetime across France, yet my mind and the digging paranoia inside me wouldn't let me forget the truth.

I rolled our suitcases along behind me, listening to the click-clack of Rachael's heeled boots on the marble floor. Outside the station, we caught a cab and I asked the driver to take us to the nearest hotel, anxious to get settled in and walk. I could walk for miles. My mind worked best when I was moving.

Lost inside my head, wondering where Nadia could be, I came back to the present when the cab lurched to a stop and Rachael let out a small chuckle beside me.

The hotel was a disaster. Small and in disrepair with white paint peeling from the blocks of stone, which looked as if they would fall in against one another at any moment. Faded black awnings drooped over the windows. I regretted not being more specific about our hospitality needs. "It looks like a flea-infested rat trap."

Rachael grinned and took my hand. "Something about it reminds me of Turtle Tear. It needs someone to take care of it." She pointed to a stone barn barely standing in the distance. "This old farmhouse is a piece of Gothic history. I can picture it how it once was. Too bad there isn't someone like you to revive it to its original glory."

I tucked her compliment away, knowing *she* was the one who'd saved Turtle Tear, and smiled. "Maybe someone will come along. For now, looks like we'll be roughing it."

"We've survived worse." She leaned over and kissed my cheek.

We had survived worse conditions, and our time together with only candlelight and a hotel in ruins was the best of my life.

The wooden stairs up to the porch creaked under our feet. I knew enough French to read the small, carved sign hanging beside the door: *Mama and Papa Renault's Inn*. If I had to guess, the wizened old man rocking in the chair at the end of the porch, smoking a pipe, was Papa. The old man smiled—not a tooth in his head—and waved us inside. *"Bonjour!"* he called, blowing smoke around his bald, wrinkled head.

"Bonjour," Rachael replied, grinning and taking in our surroundings. I could see the wheels turning in her brain. She was itching to get her hands on this place. The Louvre held little interest for my girl, but dirt, grime, and warped boards put a fire in her eyes.

I smiled to myself, taking pride in knowing her so well, at being the one to recognize what was in her heart and mind. I wondered if anyone knew her as well as I did. I doubted it.

I hoped not.

I wanted to be the only one she let see into the dark corners of herself, the ones she only revealed in our most intimate moments when she couldn't hide her wants and desires, her most cherished memories and longings.

When it came to Rachael, I was a greedy, selfish man. I wanted all of her, every little bit, all to myself.

A plump woman in a plaid dress draped in a white apron with her gray hair pinned on top of her head greeted us inside. Fortunately, the cab driver was right behind us, hoisting our luggage up the porch stairs, and could convey our request for a room, the length of our stay undetermined.

I didn't think that would be an issue, considering the state of the inn and the lack of other patrons. Despite the rundown appearance outside and the desperate need for updating inside, the inn was well kept and looked to be clean.

The old woman chattered at us in rapid French, of which I caught maybe two words, and then she turned and shouted over her shoulder. "Paul!"

After a moment, a tall young man about MJ's age—early twenties—strode through a doorway to where I believed the kitchen would be, smiled, and grasped our luggage.

The proprietress pointed up the stairs to where Paul was hauling our suitcases and said, "Two. Room two," in French-accented English.

"Perfect." I nodded my thanks, unable to recall the basics of the language and wishing I'd had time to brush up on it before our trip.

The woman ushered us through a large sitting room and through a pair of doors out onto a flagstone patio. That was when I realized the beauty of Mama and Papa Renault's Inn.

Acres of grapevines sprawled out before us over the hillside. Behind the ancient barn, the trees struggled to hold on to fall leaves of the most vibrant reds and oranges I'd ever seen. The sky overhead was a brilliant blue, so bright it hurt my eyes.

While I marveled at our surroundings, Rachael took a seat at a battered picnic table and our hostess brought out wine, grapes, and cheese. At some time, Papa Renault had found his way around back and sat under a nearby tree smoking and watching us.

"I think you're in love," Rachael said, pouring me a glass of white wine. "Funny how it sneaks up on you like that."

She was teasing, but it wasn't far from how I felt. "It's no Turtle Tear," I said, stepping over the bench and sitting across from her. "But there's something about it."

Rachael lifted her glass. "I think we were brought here for a reason. Someday we'll know what it is."

I lifted my glass and clinked it against hers. She had an old soul that spoke to mine. "Here's to someday." The crisp, sweet wine tingled on my tongue, holding the promise of good things to come.

Ten

Rachael

My greatest weakness was my lack of patience. At the Renaults' inn, it was easy to sit back, relax, and forget why we were in France, but when it all rushed back, it came with resentment. I wanted to enjoy this experience with Merrick, and Nadia had taken that from me. Even if she was the very reason we were in Nice in the first place.

I ran my hand along the grape leaves as Merrick and I walked between two rows. "Reminds me of the key lime orchard at Turtle Tear," I said. I couldn't help the comparisons. It was like a French version of my favorite place on earth.

"Uh-huh," he said, distracted.

I could only wait so long and it had been long enough. "Call her," I said. "Nadia. Call her and find out where they are."

"I told you, I can't do that."

"*I* did and here we are. You know if you'd left it up to her, we'd still be sitting in Paris going crazy. Probably ready to kill each other."

He stopped short and turned to me. "So you were right.

Is that what you want to hear, Rachael? You were right and I was wrong."

Jesus, there he went again. I just wanted him to move the process along. "No, Merrick. I—"

"You what? You think I'm stupid for wanting to trust Nadia. You think she's playing me. Well, maybe she is. I don't know what to think or what to do." He threw his hands in the air and started walking again.

I grabbed his arm. "Don't be an ass. And don't you dare walk away from me."

He ran his hands through his hair in frustration. "I don't know what you want from me, Rachael. I'm going on instinct here."

I put my hands on his hips and stepped in to him. "I want you to let me help. You can't keep me uninvolved. I'm *involved*! I'm here. I can't just follow you around like a lap-dog. I get a say in this, don't I? I thought we were a team."

Merrick grasped my shoulders and pushed me back a step, drilling his eyes into mine. "No. You don't get a say in this. You get to stay as far away from Enzo as possible. You're here so I can have you with me and know where you are at all times."

"Are you fucking kidding me?" My head was about to explode. "I guess that's my answer. We're not a team. There's still you—in control, doing what you want—and I should just go along with it and like it. Well, guess what? I won't do it!"

I pivoted from his angered and bewildered expression

and yanked a handful of grape leaves from a vine. Behind me, I heard him groan. "Rachael—"

"No!" I turned on him, pounded a fist against his chest. "If I'm not a part of this, then I'm not a part of your life and I guess there's no *us* at all, is there?"

Merrick's expression went blank, turned to stone. "You don't know what it's like." He ran a hand down his face and began to pace. "I have a daughter who needs me." He jolted to a halt and captured my eyes. "I can't expect you to understand."

My throat constricted in anger. "Because I don't have kids? Because you're the expert now?"

His forehead creased, brows knit. "I don't claim to be an expert, but I never felt this way before I knew I was a father." He pressed his hand to his chest. "They're a part of me. I won't turn my back on them."

"I never asked you to."

The set, determined look in his eyes frightened me. "Don't ever make me choose."

His words struck me so hard, I stumbled backward. He caught me by the arm. The world spun around me, all grapevines, sunlight, and bright blue sky—an absolute contradiction to the bleak blackness overtaking me.

He wouldn't choose me. I would forever be relegated to third best in his life. I'd either accept it, or…or it was over.

Eleven

Merrick

She pulled her arm from my grasp and strode away from me.

I let her go.

I should've never said that.

There was nothing I wanted more than to go to her and take every word back. But I couldn't. No matter how much I loved her—because I loved her—I needed her to understand my life now. I was a father. I had responsibility and I would never turn away from one of my kids asking for my help, even Nadia.

The justification didn't keep my gut from feeling like it was being torn out and my chest from being ripped open.

With my head so full of churning thoughts, it might have taken fifteen minutes or fifteen hours to get back to the inn.

I'd known all along, my happiness was fleeting. Like holding water in my hand, it slipped through my fingers.

The pain was like nothing I'd ever experienced. Emotional torture. My throat was thick and ached with unshed tears, my chest heavy, my lungs struggling to take in air.

Why couldn't she understand what I felt? How much I had to make up for with MJ and Nadia.

No, MJ wasn't the issue. Rachael loved MJ. It was Nadia she didn't like or trust.

Hell, I wasn't sure I trusted her either, but as her father, it wasn't really an option to turn away. I'd never do that.

Jesus, what was I supposed to do? Never in a million years would I have thought this would come between me and Rachael.

Stepping inside the patio doors and ambling to the front of the inn, I spotted Paul, the young man who had taken our bags to our room, sitting at a small desk beside the front door. He glanced up as I stopped in front of him. "The woman I'm with," I said, "did she come inside?"

"Non." Paul studied my face. I knew I couldn't hide my complete anguish.

I nodded, unable to speak. Upstairs, I opened the door to our room. I sank down on the foot of the bed and let my head fall into my hands.

My Rachael...would she be mine much longer? Could she accept me as a father, or would this be the end of us?

The idea of losing her struck me like a hammer blow to the heart.

What if I never slid that ring on her finger? Never saw her walking toward me down the aisle? Never celebrated an anniversary, a childbirth, even a Christmas?

The nevers were endless. I couldn't let this happen to us.

At the foreign sensation of warm, wet tears slipping down my cheeks, I became completely unhinged. I couldn't remember the last time I'd cried and now I wasn't sure I'd ever stop.

The door opened slowly and Rachael stepped in. I lifted my eyes from her feet to her mascara-streaked face. "Why are you doing this to us?" she whispered.

We stared at each other, miserable, desperate, and devastated.

"I need you to accept me for who I am now." My voice was raw and ragged.

"You're shutting me out. How can I accept something you won't let me be a part of? Don't you understand that?"

I let out a harsh laugh and hoisted my heavy soul off the bed. "Don't *I* understand that?" I gripped her shoulders and pulled her against me. "I don't even know how to be a part of this yet, how—"

"Try," she said, her voice muffled against my chest. "Promise me!" She pounded her fists against my shoulders. "Don't you love me? Don't you want to be with me?"

"Don't I want to be with you?" I let out a rattling breath. "How can you doubt how much I love you?"

She stepped back from me, wrapping her arms around herself. "You told me I couldn't be part of your decisions." She sniffled and sobbed. "You've shut me out of your life."

"You know why. It has nothing to do with how much I love you." Watching her turn in on herself, away from me, cowering in her own arms, crying like a helpless, wounded child, it was more than I could take. "Jesus, you have to know I love you more than my own life, Rachael." I tried to hold her, but she pulled away.

"How would I know that?" She wouldn't look at me. Tears dripped from her downturned face to the hardwood floor.

It was time—it couldn't wait another second—damn it all to hell. "This wasn't the way I wanted to do this." I strode across the room to my suitcase, dug in the inside pocket, and pulled out the black ring box. "Look at me, Rachael."

She lifted her eyes and I held up the box. "I bought this in Atlanta months ago." I shook my head and walked toward her.

Rachael wiped her cheeks, but couldn't keep up with the stream of tears. Her eyes tilted in confusion. "I don't understand."

I took her hand and guided her down onto the bed to sit beside me. "I couldn't buy you a ring in that shop yesterday, Rachael, because I already had one. I've been carrying it around with me, loving the feel of it in my pocket, knowing it would be on your finger someday, but fighting off every urge to give it to you, to beg you to be with me forever."

Overwhelmed, she covered her open mouth with her hand. She blinked tear after tear out of her welling eyes. "I don't—why? Why didn't you want to ask me?"

"I do! My God, I do. I wanted to make sure you had enough time to come to terms with things. You didn't sign up for a package deal when we met. I didn't want you to say yes and regret it, or say no and slay me on the spot. I didn't want you to feel like you had to because of Turtle Tear, or because of everything going on. I didn't want a pity acceptance when I proposed."

"A pity acceptance?" She sounded so bewildered, I reached out and stroked her hair to comfort her, half expecting her to flinch or back away, but she didn't.

"It had to be perfect," I said. "The perfect time. The perfect place. But I can't let you think I don't love you with every piece of me. Every single cell inside of me."

I slowly slid off the bed, down onto one knee, and opened the ring box. I admired it, sparkling in its nest of velvet. I'd peeked in the box a million times, wondering if it was good enough for her, if she'd like it. As my eyes lifted to hers, wide and overwhelmed, I had my answer.

"Rachael, this was supposed to come when we were back at home. I wanted to do this on the deck of the tree house on one of those mornings when the herons fly over and the scent of the sweet key limes fills the air, but like always, my gut instinct took over, I messed everything up, made you doubt me, and now has to be the time." I reached up and put my hand over her eyes. "Close your eyes for me. Pretend we're home."

She took my hand away and held it in hers, threading our fingers together. "I don't want to pretend I'm anywhere but here. This is how we work. Your knee-jerk reactions are why we're together at all. This is the way it's supposed to be, Merrick. This is *our* way."

God. How could any one woman know me so well? Know exactly how to find my every insecurity and wrangle it to the ground? "Then there's only one thing left to do." I set the open ring box beside her on the bed and cradled her face in my hands. "Since the first time I saw you—no, before that, the first time I heard your voice, that determined, stubborn voice telling me how perfect you were for my project manager position—I knew I had to have you. You belonged in my life, and one way or another, I would have you."

She inhaled sharply and smiled, pressing her lips together as the tears kept flowing. I brushed them away with my thumbs. "I don't know how, or why, Rachael, but you get me like nobody ever has. You understand the circles of thought in my mind and why I do the crazy-stupid things I do."

Rachael let out a small laugh and my heart leapt. I felt myself smile and clung to the hope that I hadn't destroyed everything between us. "I want the world with you. I want what we already have and everything I see for us in the future. You're my home, Rachael, the only one I've ever had, and I want you to be my wife. Will you marry me?"

Rachael nodded, her face still held in my hands. "I want that more than anything. I'd marry you this second if I could." She started laughing and crying at the same time. "This is the most emotionally draining trip I've ever taken."

I began to laugh with her, plucked the ring out of the box, stood, and pulled her up into my arms. "You just signed on for a lifetime on this roller coaster, so buckle in." I took her left hand and slipped the diamond ring on her finger. "I promise to be the best husband I can be until the day I die."

Rachael grinned and pecked my lips. "I promise to hold you to it."

Taking her hand, I lifted the ring to my lips and, like she taught me, sealed my promise with a kiss.

Twelve

Rachael

I examined my engagement ring with blurry, gritty eyes, strained and burning from all of my crying. The diamond was large but not pretentious, oval, resting in an antique filigree setting of what I figured was platinum. It was breathtaking.

My heart expanded and the salty wetness began to pool in my eyes again as I looked up at Merrick.

"It's similar to Ingrid Weston's ring," he said, taking my hand and admiring the beautiful stone. "In the photo of her and Archibald on their family tree, her ring looks a little bit like this." He brushed a strand of hair back from my face and tucked it behind my ear. "They brought us together. I wanted to acknowledge that in your ring, but it had to be all yours, too—ours. Just ours."

Ingrid Burkhart Weston was the original matron of Turtle Tear. I recited the love story between her and her husband Archibald to Merrick during our interview. Ingrid's parents forbade her to be with Archibald, so he climbed a ladder to her window and whisked her away to Turtle Tear. When I turned down the project manager position with Rocha Enterprises to stay at home with my mother—what she wanted, not what I wanted—Merrick wouldn't let me sacrifice my desire to lead the renovation of the hotel. Being the impulsive, stubborn man that he is, he kidnapped me, although we like to refer to it as whisking me away to Turtle Tear as Archibald did with Ingrid. Waking up tied to a bed in the ruins of an historic hotel with a guilt-ridden man who has no interest in harming you, only talking you into accepting a position with his company, is insane, and at the same time, it was our perfect start.

Merrick slipped the ring from my finger and held it up so I could see the inside edge of the band, where a small turtle was engraved along with the words: *Forever My Home and Heart—M.*

Speechless and overwhelmed, I stood on tiptoe, tears falling freely, reaching for his lips as he slid the ring back on my finger. "That smile," he said before I could kiss him, "it's what I live for."

"You could've been getting a lot more smiles if you would've just given me the damn ring sooner," I teased, and bit his bottom lip.

"Ouch!" Merrick chuckled and grabbed me, dipping me back and pressing his soft, demanding lips to mine. I inhaled deeply through my nose, closing my eyes and relaxing into his kiss, feeling secure in his arms. I ran my hands up over his strong shoulders and twined my fingers in his hair. The ring felt so foreign, yet so…anticipated, on my finger. Despite what had brought the proposal about, this moment was perfect and I'd never forget it.

Before I knew what was happening, I was airborne and came down on the bed with a soft bounce. Merrick pounced and held himself over me with a devious glint in his eye. "Now, Ms. DeSalvo, will you stop picking fights with me, or do I have to take drastic measures?"

A giggle bubbled up from my stomach as desire flamed between my legs. I reached down and grasped the bulge behind his zipper. "I'm in need of drastic measures, Mr. Rocha. Very drastic measures."

"Mmm. You're in for it now, woman." He flicked open the button on my jeans and unzipped them. As he scooted down the bed, tugging my pants down, I grasped the hem of his shirt and pulled it off over his head.

With one deft yank, my jeans and underwear were swept off and tossed to the floor. Merrick splayed his fingers across the inside of my thighs and pushed them far apart. His dark eyes smoldered as he gazed up at me. "I owe you a million earth-shattering orgasms for what I put you through today. I'm so sorry. I only wanted—"

I shoved his face between my legs, muffling his words. "Start with the drastic measures already!" The last thing I wanted was to rehash what was now behind us. We had a beautiful future to start.

Merrick laughed, his hot breath and vibrating lips against my delicate flesh. I arched my back and ran my nails over his scalp. "You asked for it," he whispered, blowing down my center.

Hell yes, I asked for it. I'd beg for it if I had to. I was so far gone, addicted to this man between my legs, I'd suffer a serious withdrawal without him. But he was mine. One hundred percent mine. My fiancé. Soon to be my husband. Mine and nobody else's forever.

Well, except MJ and Nadia's...

He spread me open with his fingers and licked me from my bottom to the tip, where he pressed his tongue firmly against the tiny, miraculous nerves that sent me through the ceiling. Letting out heavy pants of breath, I watched him, caught his eyes and wicked smirk as he did it a second time.

God, how did I get so lucky? His broad shoulders flexed against my legs, and his long fingers swirled gently, replacing his tongue as he lowered his eyes, studying me. "Beautiful," he whispered. "All I ever want."

He latched his lips on to me, probing me with his tongue and sucking gently, then harder. There was no stopping the rush, the build, the inevitable explosion. I closed my eyes, gave myself over to Merrick completely, and let it come with such force, I cried out, head thrown back, fists gripping his hair. "Merrick, Merrick, Merrick," I found myself whimpering when I came back from my out-of-body experience.

He took my hand, loosening it from his hair, and sat up on his knees. "Come here."

Slack-boned and limp-muscled, I let him pull me up. He slipped both hands under my butt and lifted me up the incline of his thighs. I wrapped my arms around his neck, pressing my breasts against his chest, and slid my tongue between his lips. Kissing this man, tasting him—and me on him—exploring him, was my lifeblood. I thrived on being this close—could never get close enough.

We held each other and kissed like it was the first time . . . the last time. His hands squeezed my behind, pushing his hard length against me. I hooked my ankles behind him and let my hands roam over his shoulders, up the sides of his face, and down his back with suppressed urgency. I didn't want to rush it, but could barely hold myself back.

He kissed my collarbone, my neck, and under my ear before whispering, "Wife. I like how that sounds. Wife."

I couldn't suppress a delighted laugh. "I like how it sounds, too. Husband. That has a nice ring to it, don't you think?"

"I do. Hmm . . . I do. I do, I do." Merrick chuckled and kissed my cheek, my forehead, my nose. "Do you want a baby?"

Shocked, I backed away enough to look into his eyes. "Not tonight." I laughed. "Maybe someday. Do you?"

His head tilted slightly as he considered it. His lips curved into a slight smile. "I think I do, Rachael. Something about imagining you with our baby makes me want it to be real."

I pressed my forehead to his so we were nose to nose. "You will be a wonderful father. You've already had a little practice after all."

He threaded his fingers through my hair and held my head in his hands. "Next time I'll be around for all of it."

I grinned and tightened my thighs around his waist. “You couldn’t get away if you tried.”

Merrick lifted me and settled me down onto him, easing gently into me. I let my head fall back and moaned. “I’d never try,” he whispered against my throat.

We rocked wordlessly, soundlessly, unhurried. He lifted and lowered me in a gentle, easy rhythm, building pressure inside me so sweet, my eyes stung with tears. Overwhelmingly happy tears.

It was happening. Merrick and I were engaged. The ring on my finger promised we would be married soon. He wanted a baby. It was unreal to me that he’d asked. We’d never spoken of it—of any of it—but I should’ve known we’d be on the same page. We always were when all of the misunderstanding was stripped away and it was just the two of us, bare to the blinding white truth.

Thirteen

Merrick

Rachael clenched my shoulders tighter and increased her pace, rising and falling on me faster and faster. I felt her tighten and twitch around me. "Yes," she whispered between moans. I couldn't hold on much longer. She'd take me with her any second.

I trained my gaze on her face, knowing exactly how her brows would bunch together over her closed eyes. She'd cry out and then her mouth would remain open, soundless, widening as a rush of breath came out before a whimper. I loved giving her that expression, hearing the ecstasy in her moans and seeing it when she was silently riding the last of the wave.

God, she was so tight. So hot and wet. She gritted her teeth and rode me hard, determined to get what she wanted. What she needed. "Take it," I whispered. I thumbed her nipples, groaning as she rose even higher and slammed down onto me.

If she didn't come fast, I was going to throw her on her back and make her come. This was torture of the most amazing kind, but I needed to explode inside her and feel the spasms of her orgasm around my cock. "Come for me, baby."

She was a woman possessed. Her eyes pierced mine, begging without a word as her hips ground against mine, seeking, eager, desperate to find release. Gently, I pushed her a hand's-width away from my body and eased my palm down between us, gliding over her sweat-dampened skin. My thumb slipped between her slick folds and zeroed in on the sweet spot that would give her what she needed. I rubbed her quickly, firmly, and she bucked up from my lap with her head thrown back. "Right there," she cried, impaling herself back down onto me. "Yes, Merrick. Right there."

She rode me fast and hard as I worked her with my thumb, taking a hard, pebbled nipple into my mouth and sucking it, nipping it with my teeth. She groaned and ran her nails across my back. "Yes—that—oh God!"

Her muscles gripped around me, pulsing in perfect spasms. My own throbbing started and I let it come, sweeping over me like a tidal wave. Our bodies pressed tight, grinding, contracting, taking and giving in perfect unison. I wove my fingers in her hair and held her to me tightly before laying her back on the bed and easing down on top of her.

I was careful not to lower my entire weight onto her, but I had to feel her under me and kiss her breathless mouth. She was so delicate, so soft and vulnerable. I couldn't believe someone would open herself to me so completely, but every time we made love, I was amazed once again how she gave herself entirely.

I traced a line from her temple to her chin, her eyes still closed. She couldn't ever know what she meant to me—what losing her now would do to me.

And she'd agreed to be my wife.

Now that it was settled and I'd asked and she'd accepted, I knew the reason I'd put off asking, and it had nothing to do with giving her time. It was my own fear and insecurity that she'd say no.

I knew she loved me, but promising me the rest of her life was a whole different story. I came with baggage. With issues—so many issues. She took them all in stride and with grace, but would she tire of it?

I had to get better—be better—for her. I wanted to be the best husband she could ever imagine. The thought panicked me. Could I do it?

I shifted and Rachael opened her eyes. "Where are you going?" She grabbed my hips to keep me top of her. "Stay inside me."

Chuckling, I kissed her forehead. "Trust me, if I could have myself surgically attached, I'd do it."

I smoothed her eyebrow and kissed her, reveling in her soft, warm lips parting for me, her tongue seeking mine, her quiet moan.

I let my lips stray to the corner of her mouth, her cheek, her jaw, and down her neck. "The only place you're ever going to be is with me."

She grasped my face in her hands and ran the tip of her nose down the bridge of mine. "And you with me."

"I already told you, I'd be surgically attached if I could." I thrust my hips, proving my point.

Rachael inhaled deeply and smiled. "Mmm. Again, my handsome fiancé?" She spread her legs wider, wrapping them around my waist.

I ground my hips against hers. "Again. And again and again. A lifetime of *agains*." I took her hands, kissed her ring, and pinned her arms over her head. "Now it's my turn to be on top."

She dug her heels into the mattress and lifted her hips up to meet mine. "Bring it on, Mr. Rocha. You know I can take anything you dish out."

"Can you?" I grinned, knowing she could. There wasn't a more perfect woman for me on earth.

"Try me," she said, arching into me, egging me on.

I let her hands go and slipped my arms around her, lowering into her and rocking gently. Making slow, sweet love to her was all I wanted.

She giggled softly in my ear. "I love you, Merrick."

"You must, and that makes me the luckiest man in the world." I lowered my forehead against hers and closed my eyes, letting the scent of her warm skin and our coming together fill me. "I love you, too, Rachael."

Fourteen

Rachael

Prisms of light reflected off my diamond and shot rainbows through my glass of water. I admired the swirling colors before picking up the sweating glass and taking a deep drink.

It was nearly noon and an unseasonably hot day for fall, making me wish I'd brought something lightweight to wear. A few stray grapes lay on a plate beside the remnants of cheese and crusty bread that Mama Renault had brought out for us for a midmorning snack. I had a feeling I'd turn into a grape before leaving the inn, I'd eaten so many.

Merrick had disappeared with the Renaults' son, Paul, into the cockeyed stone barn that Mama had assured me was safe and not about to fall down around them despite its decrepit appearance. That was over an hour ago.

I was just about to get up and go inside when a high-pitched whine overlapped by a deep-chested rumble drew my attention to the barn. The double doors where shoved open by Paul and out rode Merrick on an ancient, dark green and black motorcycle. Both men were grinning ear to ear.

Merrick turned and gunned the engine, taking off like a bullet down the dirt path that led behind the barn. Paul put a hand up to shade his eyes as he watched. My heart sputtered and pounded. I hated motorcycles. Something so... open and precariously balanced shouldn't go that fast. Seeing Merrick's dark hair whipping around his head, I gritted my teeth to rein in my anger at him for not wearing a helmet.

Wrapping my arms around myself, I trained my ears on the distant engine and tried to keep calm. Shouldn't he ask me how I feel about him riding a motorcycle? We were engaged now after all.

Maybe that wasn't how it worked. I'd never been engaged before, so I had no idea what I should expect from him. But staying alive at least until the wedding should be a given!

Walking toward me, Paul closed the distance between us with long, eloquent strides. "He come around," he said with a decent grasp of English, pointing to the opposite side of the vineyard.

True to Paul's claim, a couple minutes later, the whine-rumble of the motorcycle could be heard coming up the far side of the grapevines. Paul put a hand in the air, waved it back and forth, and began to laugh. "He's good. Good driver."

"He's something," I muttered, rising on tiptoe to get a better view. "If he kills himself, I'll kill him."

There he was, Merrick Rocha, king of the road, or the

Renault Vineyard at least, pumping a fist in the air and laughing into the wind. It was the happiest I had seen him—out of our bed—in weeks. With a swift pang in my gut, I held my left hand out and glimpsed at the sparkling diamond on my finger.

There'd been so much stress and animosity between us lately. A ring doesn't make it all disappear. There were issues we had to face and work through. He had to see me as a partner, someone to make decisions with, not around. I knew he was used to being the man in charge, but if he was looking for a meek woman who would sit back and let him rule, he picked the wrong woman.

Mama Renault bustled out the patio door chatting rapid-fire French to Paul while lifting both hands to shade her eyes, looking toward Merrick on the motorcycle. Before Paul had a chance to respond, she grasped my arm and cried out, "Oh! Papa's motorcycle!" Then began to laugh and clap her hands.

"Papa can't ride," Paul explained. "Too old."

"You like to ride?" Mama asked me, gesturing enthusiastically at the quickly approaching bike. "Go for a ride."

"No. I don't like to ride," I said, taking a step back.

Merrick pulled up to the patio and lowered his feet to the ground to brace the bike. It idled like the purr of a wild cat just freed from the zoo. He patted the seat behind him, grinning at me like a madman. "Hop on!"

He *was* mad to think I'd go anywhere near that thing. "No way."

"Come on. You can hold on to me. There's a lake way down past the vineyard I want you to see. It's beautiful." He cocked one brow and shot me his dimpled Rocha smile. "Please?"

In light of my need to assert myself and enforce my opinions, I wanted to plant my ass firmly on the picnic table bench and refuse to budge, but the warm gush of emotions flowing through my chest at the sight of him, excited, filled to bursting with exuberance and wanting to share that feeling with me, had me giving in.

I sighed. "Fine, but if you kill me, I'll never forgive you."

He laughed as I swung a leg over the seat and wrapped my arms around his waist. "You'll haunt me for the rest of my life alive *or* dead." He lifted my hand and kissed it. "I prefer you breathing, though." Leaning back, he turned his head to whisper in my ear, "I lied. I prefer you breathless underneath me. Hold on tight."

We took off with a jolt and I buried my face against his back. The wind whipped my hair around in tangles, and the seat sent vibrations through my entire body. I eased my eyes away from Merrick and glanced over his shoulder.

My breath caught in my throat at the sight of endless green hills and valleys with their cut-out fields like a patchwork quilt, some dotted in reds, yellows, and purples of autumn flowers, some striped by vineyards. The tall, leaning stone barn stood sentry, watching over the Renault property.

Merrick pointed to a lake, just visible up ahead. The

banks were clogged with water weeds, a small blue wooden boat bobbed just off the shore, and an old farmhouse sat, squat and square, at the water's edge, like a bloated fat toad. The holes in the thatched roof, broken windows, and general disrepair spoke of abandonment from long ago.

Merrick slowed and stopped, lowering his feet to the ground, then turned the bike's engine off. "What do you think?"

"It's amazing." I eased off the bike, eyes locked on the house. I felt my creativity itching to escape onto design boards.

He laughed and propped the bike up before kicking his leg over and following me toward the water. "I mean the motorcycle. I knew you'd like the house."

I shoved my windblown hair back, trying to conceal a smile. "It's not as terrible as I thought."

"That's a rare vintage Harley-Davidson." He took my hand and helped me into the little blue boat.

"It's loud." I sat and watched him climb in and push us off the bank with an oar. He looked better than he had in a long time. Hair blown back, sun on his face, smile in his eyes. If the bike did this for him, he could have twenty of the damn things.

"I was thinking of making Paul an offer for it." One of his brows cocked, testing me. "I could get it shipped to Turtle Tear, ride it around the island. You have to admit it's a lot more fun that a golf cart. Plus, Beck would go insane over it."

At that, he seemed to shut down, turning to face the water, chin dropped, forehead creased. Something was going on. "Merrick?" I reached out and touched his knee. "I think that sounds like a great idea."

He covered my hand with his. A sad smile crossed his lips. "Beck's gone. Went back to Nebraska."

"What? Why?"

"I fired him. You've heard him play that cello. That's what he was meant to do. His life's been stranded on that island for long enough."

I couldn't believe what I was hearing. "But he moved on from playing professionally. He didn't want to do that anymore. Just because he dug it out and started playing again doesn't mean he wasn't happy with what he was doing on the island. He was content with his life how it was, Merrick. How could you do that?"

"Being content isn't good enough. He deserves more."

Every second brought me more and more anger. I pulled my hand from his knee and sat up straight. "You have to stop playing dictator. You don't always get to choose what happens to the people in your life. Let us choose!"

Confusion swept over his features. "Dictator? That's what you think of me? First, I'm a fool for chasing down Nadia, now I'm a dictator? Why the hell would you agree to marry me if you think those things?"

I clenched my fists in rage. "Why is it all or nothing with you? I can love you without you having to be perfect! I'm not perfect! Do you not love me despite my flaws?"

He blinked a few times, narrowing his eyes. "You are perfect. Perfect for me. I'm sorry I'm not perfect for you."

"You are perfect *for me*, but nobody's perfect." We sat in silence in the center of the lake. The deep blue fall sky reflected off the water, surrounding us, and the sun warmed the tops of our heads. I wondered what was happening to us. Was this what we became when the newness of our relationship wore off?

"What now, Rach?" he asked, sweeping his fingertips in the water. "All we've done since we got here is drive each other nuts."

I watched the water ripple. "And get engaged. Makes sense, doesn't it?"

He looked up at me and grinned. "For us? Makes complete sense."

I took a deep breath and launched the words that had to be spoken out of my mouth. "We give it one more day, Merrick, then you call Nadia and tell her to meet us at the airport. This is ridiculous. She's lived almost twenty-one years without you. She's not a child. You've opened your home to her. You don't need to chase her down and make her come. She'll be there when she wants to be."

Merrick smacked his hand down into the water. "Enzo—"

"He's *not* holding her hostage! Is he? She's just reluctant to leave him and Gina for whatever reason. We'll find out what that reason is when she's ready to tell us." I grasped my upper arms, trying not to shiver from the nervous energy rushing through me from arguing. "One more day, okay?"

Merrick shoved his fingers through his hair, tugging at the ends. He didn't answer, just paddled us back to shore.

All I could do was pray we got through this together and everything would be back to normal with us once we were home at Turtle Tear.

Fifteen

Merrick

Tough love. That was what Rachael was giving me. Did I blame her? Hell, not really. Everything she said was true. We'd fought this entire trip. I was taking my stress and all the pressure I put on myself to be the father I always should have been out on her.

It wasn't fair.

I turned to her when we reached the motorcycle. "Fine. One day. Then we leave." It was all the consolation I was able to muster at the moment. The ride back would clear my mind—I hoped. We had to get past this somehow.

She held me tight, her thighs squeezing me as firmly as her arms. I wished we had helmets. I was never afraid of getting hurt before her. Before MJ and Nadia. Nobody would've cared anyway if I had. But it was different now. Rachael would care. No matter our differences, she loved me and I loved her. She'd be devastated without me, and I wouldn't want to live a second of my life without her.

I accelerated across the bottom of the vineyard, making my way to the other side of the Renault property. Was I really that controlling? I'd never thought I was, but considering how Rachael and I started and everything she'd pointed out to me today, the proof was right there—I was kind of a dictator. Here all along I thought the things I did were helping the people I cared about. But I could see now how not giving them a choice to determine their own fate was taking charge of their lives and I had no right to do that.

I had to let go. Not completely, but enough to give them room to make mistakes—or what I believed were mistakes. Maybe they didn't consider them mistakes.

God, I needed a therapist.

Or maybe just the love of a good woman—the one behind me squeezing me to death.

If anyone could knock some sense into me, it was Rachael. I chuckled to myself, letting the wind and sun and amazing landscape around us soak into my brain and drown what I couldn't control.

One more day. If Nadia wanted to come to Turtle Tear, she would, just like Rachael had said.

I pulled up to the back patio at the inn and turned off the bike. Mama and Paul were sitting at the picnic table drinking lemonade. Papa was smoking under a tree at the corner of the house, watching. I nodded to him. "Great bike."

Papa nodded and blew out a puff of smoke.

Rachael got off and shook out her legs. "Lots of vibration."

I winked at her, knowing she'd get the innuendo I took from her words. She smirked.

I strode over and sat down next to Paul. "How much would your father sell it for?"

Mama's hands shot into the air. *"Non, non,"* she said, a big smile on her face. "A gift. *Pour vos fiançailles.* Papa insists."

Rachael's eyes went wide across the table. This was way too generous to accept. A vintage Harley from strangers? I shook my head, making eye contact with the old man under the tree. "I appreciate the gesture, but I can't accept it as a gift. I'd be happy to pay you for it, though."

Mama began speaking to Papa in French, gesturing toward me. The man waved a hand and took his pipe from his mouth to utter, *"Je ne le veux pas."*

"He says he doesn't want it," Paul said.

"Take it!" Mama said, flinging her open palm out toward the bike, smiling and nodding.

Rachael shrugged. Her lips quirked at the ends as if to say, why not? I wasn't comfortable with it, but had an idea of how I'd repay Mr. Renault in the future. "Okay. Thank you. It's a wonderful gift." I reached across the table and squeezed Mama's hand. She patted mine and Paul smacked me on the back.

The past few days I had been thrown out of my element. Not that I wasn't used to traveling to different countries and meeting new people, but not having any idea where to be or what to do next made me as unsteady as walking a tightrope. A tightrope with no net. I didn't like not being able to formulate a plan, even a half-assed one, that would get me the result I wanted. Letting go of control was the foreign element to this journey and maybe that was what fate had in store for me all along.

My one day was almost up. We'd gotten up early and ridden the motorcycle into the nearby village. I'd sent a text message to Nadia's number telling her to meet us at the inn if she could, and that we would be at the airport departing at 10 p.m., the latest flight I could book. I hadn't heard back.

"This looks like a picture," Rachael said, admiring the baskets full of apples, pears, and figs lined up for sale on a farmer's cart. "It's so quaint, like something out of the past. I didn't think places like this existed anymore."

"I know." I strolled over to the basket of fall apples and picked one up. "The place time forgot."

The narrow cobblestone street led to a white, steepled church. Tall, brick buildings loomed over them with windows shuttered from the late-day sun. A bird was singing somewhere out of sight, its soprano voice floating in and out on the breeze.

I hadn't been so content in months. With the decision about Nadia made and executed, I could just exist. Here. Now. And enjoy the time I had with my beautiful fiancée.

I pointed to the church. "Want to go in and get hitched?"

She laughed. "Get hitched? Only if we can tie cans to the back of the Harley on our way back to the inn."

"Done." I scooped her up in my arms and started down the street. Her peals of laughter were contagious, and soon

I was lost to the swell of happiness in my chest, letting it out loudly.

"Put me down!" she said, and smacked her lips against mine in a hard, wet kiss.

"Oh, no. When I proposed, you said you'd marry me in a second if you could. So what's wrong with right now?" I spun her around in a circle, making her laugh again. Her hair flew out behind her, the light brown, caramel-colored strands catching the sun. She was so beautiful, sometimes I couldn't believe she was really mine.

"Nobody's here with us! My mom and Aunt Jan would flip out if I came back from France married. I haven't even called to tell them I'm engaged yet!"

I stopped suddenly and gave her a fake glare. "Why not? Planning on changing your mind?"

"Never!" She grabbed my face between her hands and kissed me again. Her lips were cool and she smelled like crisp leaves and sweet lip balm. The way her hands held me was gentle yet possessive, her touch promising the same as her words to never let me go.

I eased her feet back onto the ground and squeezed her tight. "Fine. I'll wait. But not for long." I tucked her hair behind her ear. "Have you been thinking of a date?"

She nodded with a far-off, dreamy look in her eyes. I wished I could see the image in her mind. "The third Saturday in November. Right around Thanksgiving."

"That's perfect, because I'm so thankful for you." I ran my thumbs across her eyebrows.

"Do you think MJ would mind if we had it at the Weston Plantation?"

This took me by surprise. "You don't want it at Turtle Tear?"

"I'd love it at Turtle Tear. But I don't think there's enough room for everyone and there are no other hotels accessible to the island. I figured our guest list would be around four hundred with all of your business associates and their guests."

"That's too big." There was no way I wanted to turn our special day into some kind of circus.

She rested her palms on my shoulders. "Everyone's going to want to know who finally got you to settle down and get married, Mr. Rocha, and I intend to make sure they know."

I chuckled, loving her feisty nature. "I'll surrender to your every whim on this, Ms. DeSalvo, just know that I don't need any of the fanfare, only you saying 'I do.' "

Rachael sighed. "Turtle Tear would be nice, but I feel like a big celebration will be expected and we'd disappoint people."

Never one to care what anyone else thought, I wished for only one day she could put everyone aside and have the wedding she wanted. I'd have to work on her. There was a little time before all the preparations started. At least a *few* days.

I allowed myself a mental eye roll knowing the minute she stepped foot back on Turtle Tear, she'd fall into full wedding planning mode and I'd be stuck in the midst of it with no Beck. "Hey," I said, suddenly reminded, "do you want Beck to play his cello for the ceremony?"

"Of course!" She took me by the hand and started strolling down the little road. "I never thought I'd say it. He was so rusty playing that thing, but he seems to be right back to professional level. Not that I'm any judge of what a professional sounds like, but to my ears he qualifies." She grinned up at me. "Do you think he'll really go back to the orchestra?"

The thought of Beck in a tux playing classical music on a stage with an audience was crazy, but I could picture it. He'd played for the wedding Rachael had hosted on Turtle Tear—the hotel's first and so far only event—and nailed it. "Beck's one of those people who is comfortable doing anything. If he could transition from the orchestra to construction foreman, he can go back. I hope he does." Quickly, I added, "If he wants to."

The sun was setting, casting long shadows over a low brick wall that lined the right side of the road. The scent of meat roasting wafted out of a house on our left. My stomach growled. "We better head back, pack up, and get dinner before we need to be at the airport."

Reluctantly, Rachael stopped walking and glanced around, soaking in her last glimpse of the perfect French village tucked in between sprawling green hills. "Can we come back here sometime?"

I threaded our fingers together and kissed her hand. "As much as you want."

Her hopeful question spurred an idea that had been forming in my mind of the perfect wedding gift. Looking down at her, I knew I'd never deny her anything. Just the opposite. I would always jump through hoops, cross mountains, swim seas to give her everything she wanted and needed. I'd never known love like this before Rachael, and the fullness I felt in my chest made me want to climb up to the church steeple at the end of the road and yell my love for her at the top of my lungs for the entire world to hear.

Sixteen

Rachael

As crazy as it seemed, I couldn't wait to have the motorcycle at Turtle Tear. The day spent riding it to and from the village had me changing my mind about it, and the thought of riding it on dirt paths was a lot better than the thought of riding it at seventy miles an hour on pavement with cars, trucks, and semis whizzing past.

It started to drizzle as we ate dinner at the inn with the doors to the patio open. A chilly breeze blew in, bringing the freshness of wet grass and damp leaves to the table where we sat with Mama, Papa, and Paul.

I set my fork down, unable to eat one bite more of the delectable rosemary chicken on my plate. I wiped my mouth with my linen napkin and committed the people around me, the room, the sounds, every single thing to memory. The old inn and its owners had been the best part of our trip. I shouldn't find it surprising that the five-star hotel in Paris, the most romantic city on earth, had been where we'd done nothing but argue. The Renaults' inn was much more our style and pace of life. Like home. I'd miss this place.

After dinner, Merrick and I climbed the stairs to our room, stuffed with food and heavy-footed. We only had a little over an hour before we needed to be at the airport. I realized Merrick hadn't checked his phone since earlier in the afternoon. Maybe he'd come to the inevitable conclusion that Nadia wasn't really going to come to Turtle Tear. She wasn't planning on leaving Enzo and her mother.

It felt like being on the cusp of a revolution, like the eve before being released from prison. We would be back home after two irritatingly long plane rides and our lives would finally be back to normal. Merrick would have given his best attempt at being a father to Nadia and he'd be able to rectify his desire to make up for the past and let it go. Then we'd get married.

Stepping inside our room, I closed my eyes for a moment, savoring the thought of normalcy within my reach. I took a deep breath and smiled as I opened my eyes to find Merrick watching me. "What?" I asked.

"Something's going on inside that head of yours." He reached up and tapped my forehead.

"Just can't wait to get home. Back on track. You know?"

His face flinched for only a moment. "Have we been off track being here?"

Oh no, I wouldn't start this with him again. "No. Not off track. Being here has been...well, almost magical. This inn has something very special about it, but I'm anxious to be back home."

His expression eased. "Me, too. I don't mind traveling,

but I've done my share of it over the years. I'd rather sleep in our own bed." He ran the back of his hand down the side of my breast. "And not sleep in our own bed."

I draped my forearms over his shoulders and tipped my head back, inviting him to kiss me. He dipped his head, bringing his lips to mine, whisper close. I kissed his bottom lip, then his top before closing my mouth over his and pressing myself against him.

My tongue sought his. He tasted like the sweet tang of the apple cider we'd drunk with dinner. "I want to take a shower before we get on the plane. Join me?" I asked.

In answer, Merrick gripped the hem of my shirt and lifted it over my head. We undressed each other quickly, shedding clothes on the way to the bathroom. "Do you think you'll always want me this much?" he asked as the water ran, getting warmer by the second. He kissed my neck and rubbed his thumbs over my hardened nipples as steam began to drift out of the shower.

"I can't imagine how I couldn't." My body responded to him so eagerly—his touch, his voice, hell, just the sight of him.

We stepped inside the shower. Behind me, Merrick ran his fingertips down my slick stomach. His hands slid between my thighs, pushing them apart. His cock was hard and rigid pressing against my back. I reached behind me and grasped him in both hands as he spread my lower lips apart.

The slow, rhythmic slide of his wet fingertips back and forth and in circles was more than I could bear. He bowed his head, leaning his forehead against my crown as

I stroked him. We thrust and rocked together, panting and lost to the building ache. Throbbing and swollen with need, Merrick dipped a finger inside me. I grasped his hand, not letting him pull it out. A second finger joined the first, his other hand squeezing and pinching my nipples.

I became a woman consumed with need of this release. Desperate for the mind-numbing explosion I felt nearing the brink. With a fast push and pull, in and out, his fingers delved and pressed into me. I worked his length harder, matching his pace. Writhing against him, I felt the rush coming on and arched my back, bracing one hand against the tile wall. "Oh God." Every nerve ending sparked. I clenched my teeth. Then it hit. My body jerked, my vision blurred, I gasped for breath. Merrick was relentless, milking every last pulse from me, holding me against him while he kept me coming with deft fingers.

A second wave reared its head. "Don't stop... oh God!" I cried out as it hit me fast and hard, buckling my knees. Merrick held me up, slowing his pace until I was spent, only then freeing his fingers from inside me.

He turned me in his arms and kissed me. Breathless, I kissed him back, sliding my lips down his neck, over his collarbone, licking his stiff nipples. His cock stood tall and hard, in need of attention. I loved giving it attention.

Dropping to my knees, I took him in hand and looked up into his deep, dark, lust-hooded eyes. Making sure he watched my every move, I nuzzled his tip with my nose before running my tongue around it. He inhaled sharply, leaning toward me and pressing his hands against the wall in front of him. I nibbled his hip, teasing, testing his patience. He groaned. Smiling up at him, I brought my mouth to his cock again and slid my pursed lips down the underside, quickly licking his length all the way back up to the tip.

"Do you want me to suck you?" I asked coyly. My face and chest heated.

He grinned and chuckled, but it turned into a choke as I took him in my mouth. He barely moved. Our eyes stayed locked. I knew he was fighting the urge to thrust into me, determined to let me control his release. I took him in and out, hollowing my cheeks as I sucked. His hands fisted against the wall, his chest heaved, and finally his eyes closed. "I can't take it anymore," he said, and picked me up.

He carried me out of the shower and propped me on the vanity. I braced my hands behind me on the counter while he positioned my feet up on the edge, pushed my knees apart, and sank inside me, deep, deep inside.

Thrusting into me, Merrick ran his hands up my stomach and over my breasts. "There's something about fucking you that makes me feel more alive. Like I'm plugged into the universe with my dick inside you." He crashed his hips against mine, punctuating his words.

I couldn't do anything but whimper and moan while he plucked my nipples and squeezed my hips, angling me to get even deeper.

God, the sight of him fucking me, tall and strong, muscles contracting with each thrust of his hips, wet hair slicked back, beard grown out beyond stubble, so demanding of my body, it made my stomach quake and pulse quicken. He was beautiful, a god of a man, and he was mine.

Heat shot up my thighs, making them tremble while a fire ignited in my core. "Merrick," I whispered, sliding a hand between my legs to touch myself.

"I love it when you do that," he said. "It's so fucking hot." He hooked his arms under my knees and lifted my butt off the vanity. I leaned back on one elbow, rubbing myself desperately. It was right there, boiling under the surface. If I could just release it...

The pressure mounting inside from Merrick thrusting against my upper wall mixed with me rubbing my clit created a volcano inside me. I could feel it all the way to my toes. My orgasm gripped me tightly and didn't let go. I groaned and cried out like I was in pain, the pleasure was so overwhelming. Every muscle in my body clenched and I'd never throbbed so hard, contractions rippling through my stomach. I heard Merrick make a desperate, strangled sound, then sigh in relief as he came with a wet burst inside me.

He collapsed forward, laying his head on my heaving chest, letting my legs fall from under his arms. We breathed in unison, catching our breath. "What a way to say *au revoir* to France," he said, laving my nipple with his tongue.

He sat me up and slipped out of me. Sleepy and sated, I wrapped my arms around him and pressed my cheek to his chest. "That was my favorite part of this whole trip."

"Even better than the ring?" He pinched my butt.

"Maybe not better than that, but this was hard to top."

He laughed, but I was serious. "I don't think I could ever get tired of that," I said. "Not in a million years. I know attraction runs out between couples, but I can't see that with us. It's just so intense."

Merrick lifted my chin to look in my eyes. "Like I said, I'm plugged into the universe when I'm inside you. That can't fade. It's the most powerful feeling I could imagine."

Holding my chin between his finger and thumb, he kissed me. His passion radiated through my body. I held his head in my hands, kissing him back fiercely. I loved him so much it made my chest ache. All I could think of was getting home and becoming his wife.

Merrick was quiet as we sat at the gate waiting for our plane to board. I noticed how he kept glancing around and checking his phone. With forty-five minutes until departure, there was no hope of Nadia arriving to leave with us. I knew there never was.

"No word from her?" I asked. I hated to bring it up, even if it was so obvious, it was its own entity sitting between us. If I didn't ask, it would seem as if I didn't care. It was a touchy subject and I wasn't sure how to navigate around the subject of Nadia.

"No." He tucked his phone back into his pocket and stared straight ahead.

"Do you want to try her again?"

He shook his head. "I left her a message this morning and I asked Paul to have her contact me if she shows up at the inn."

There was nothing more he could do. We could wait around in France forever, or maybe be led to Spain or England. Who knew where Nadia would lead us next if we stayed. "She'll be in touch."

"Yeah." He gave me a brief smile that disappeared as fast as it came.

I felt terrible seeing him like this. The sooner we got home, the better.

Fifteen minutes later, we boarded first class. We were seated with our carry-ons stowed and ready to fly. I took his hand and held it, hoping to ease him at least a little. My ring sparkled and I loved how it looked on my finger while his hand was in mine. It bolstered my spirit. He would be okay. We would be more than okay and Nadia would either be in his life or not. It didn't matter.

I knew all the girl would bring us was trouble. Inviting Nadia into our lives was welcoming more pain and suffering from Enzo. Gina was an unknown variable in the more than screwed-up equation. Where she was coming from and what she was getting out of this situation were mysteries that I really didn't want to have to ponder. I hoped all three of them stayed on the other side of the Atlantic.

Seventeen

Merrick

With every mile we flew away from France, I was proving what a shitty father I was. Good fathers didn't leave their daughters across the ocean when they called for help.

Christ, I'd tried. I'd been there for a week, called her, and waited. What more could I do? Rachael's point was a valid one. Nadia was old enough to get to the airport and come to Turtle Tear if that was truly what she wanted. I'd made it clear in my message that she was welcome, that I'd pay for her flight, that she could stay as long as she wanted.

She didn't show.

What more could I do?

The flash of reflected light off Rachael's ring reminded me that I had plans, a fucking amazing life to get back to. A woman who *owned me* to marry. Going home wasn't turning my back on Nadia, even if it felt like it.

Rachael leaned her head on my shoulder. Her hair smelled like fruit and flowers. "Are you sure you want to get married at the Weston Plantation?" I knew she didn't. She was doing what was practical.

She looked up at me, beaming. "It's the most logical place to have it since there are hotels, restaurants, and shops—things to do—for people who have to travel to attend. Turtle Tear can't hold four hundred people."

"And you *want* something that big?" Rachael wasn't the type to put on an extravagant show for the benefit of others. She kept a tight group of friends and family close and they were who were important to her, not a herd of my business associates—most of whom I hadn't spoken to in years.

She shrugged. "It's a wedding. You invite everyone. That's how it's done."

"Hmm." I didn't want a wedding that was put together to make everyone happy except me and my bride. I had some thinking to do and some calls to make. I wouldn't sit back and let Rachael compromise. Practicality be damned. This day—her wedding day—would come once in her life and that was it. I'd make it amazing.

We touched down in Miami late at night. I was so used to having Beck meet me at the airport, I almost forgot there would be nobody meeting us tonight. Turtle Tear wouldn't be the same without him.

The helicopter stood ready in its designated spot. I stowed our luggage and helped Rachael into the passenger seat. She was tired, her eyes glassy. I was too, but alert enough to fly us to Turtle Tear. "Almost home." I kissed the top of her head and closed the door as she smiled through a yawn.

Both of us were quiet on the flight home, lost in our own thoughts. One of the many things I liked about being with Rachael was that we didn't need to talk all the time. Just being side by side was enough. Neither one of us needed to fill the silence.

When we touched down on the island, my assistant, Mr. Simcoe, was waiting beside the landing pad in a golf cart. The elderly man got out and limped toward us as the propellers slowed, waving. "I thought I heard a helicopter heading this way," he called.

"Good ears," I said, happy to see Mr. Simcoe so spry after his physical altercation with Enzo a few months back. "Thanks for coming down to meet us. I was afraid I'd have to lug these suitcases to the hotel on foot."

"How has everything been?" Rachael asked, coming around the front of the helicopter and rushing to give Mr. Simcoe a hug. "Is Maddie with MJ at the Weston Plantation?"

"She is. Their place is coming along nicely. Joan and Beck went to help them wrap up the west wing project, then Beck's off to Nebraska." Mr. Simcoe eyed me and pressed his lips together in a reassuring manor. "It'll be good for him to get back to his roots." He took the large tote bag off Rachael's shoulder and put it over his own. "We had an inquiry about a private business retreat. I took down the information and let the gentleman know you'd be in touch to go over pricing with him."

Rachael beamed. "Perfect! We could use another event booking!"

Pride swelled inside me. She never had to book another event on the island for as long as we lived. We didn't need the money. But she was driven, and a woman like her could never sit back and be idle, lounging on the wealth I could sustain us with. In all honesty, I liked helping her with events. We'd only had one so far, but seeing it come together gave me a sense of accomplishment I hadn't had since seeing Turtle Tear itself renovated. The wedding we'd hosted for the Nelsons, a couple renewing their vows after fifty years of marriage, was much more rewarding than my own projects had ever been. Knowing we'd provided people with cherished memories to take with them from Turtle Tear was a feeling like nothing I'd ever experienced.

Giving was much more rewarding than receiving.

Rachael had taught me that—brought giving to others into my life. I wished I had a pen and a piece of paper to write my thoughts down so I could incorporate them into my vows. I didn't want to leave out even one thing that I appreciated about her.

Mosquitoes hummed, the air was thick with humidity, and thunder cracked overhead. "Let's get to the hotel before we're poured on," Mr. Simcoe said, leading the way to the golf cart.

"I don't like that you're here alone," Rachael told Mr. Simcoe after we were in the cart and on our way down the path. "Anything could happen and nobody would be here to help."

"I'm an old man," he said, patting her leg. "When it's

my time, it's my time. Besides, I rather like being here by myself. It's peaceful."

I knew what he meant. I could breathe deeper on Turtle Tear. There was no stress. All the anxiety was gone. Well, at least when I wasn't faced with family problems, like lately with Nadia.

A sprinkle of rain wet my arm, sending a cool chill up my back. I knew I shouldn't be worrying about Nadia. I had no control over the situation, and worrying over something you have no control over is a waste. I needed to get my mind off my daughter. Glancing at Rachael's left hand, I knew exactly what to focus my attention on. "Mr. Simcoe, did you notice anything new about Rachael's left hand?"

Rachael's head snapped toward me, a huge grin on her lips.

"Look at that," Mr. Simcoe said, pulling the golf cart up to the hotel's patio. He took Rachael's hand and admired her ring. "A lovely ring for a lovely woman. Congratulations, dear." He leaned over and kissed her cheek, then held a hand out to me. "Congratulations. You've got quite the life to look forward to, son."

My eyes traveled over Rachael's face, the soft curve of her jaw, the delicate line of her cheek, her sweet nose and the mouth that she could drive me insane with. Her eyes were my favorite of her features. Soulful and expressive, dark and passionate. Rachael's eyes spoke to me without her uttering a single word. "I do have an amazing life ahead of me," I said, brushing a finger across Rachael's cheek.

She took my hand and held it. “Please don’t tell Maddie,” she said, putting a pleading hand on Mr. Simcoe’s shoulder. “I want to be the one to tell her.”

“And MJ,” I added. “Hopefully, they’ll be here next weekend.”

“I believe that’s their plan,” Mr. Simcoe said. “And don’t worry. I’d never share your news.”

The sky split with lightning and rain began to fall in buckets. The three of us darted for the shelter of the patio and hurried inside through the door to the lounge.

“I love being home,” Rachael whispered.

We lay in bed, her back to my chest, legs a tangle under the sheets, watching lightning flash and rain sheet across the sky through the window. I held her breast in my hand, her silky warm skin and rhythmic rise and fall of her chest lulling me into an almost-sleep state. But I wouldn’t let myself sleep until she did. Although she’d been exhausted on the way home, she was filled with excitement now.

“Me, too,” I whispered back, nuzzling my nose into her hair.

“I think maybe an outdoor reception at the Weston Plantation under big tents. I want a band, like an old-fashioned band to play instead of a DJ. Or maybe a band and then later at night a DJ. What do you think?”

“It sounds perfect.” I moved her hair aside and kissed the soft spot under her ear.

She turned and looked back at me. "I don't want you to agree with everything I want just because I want it. It's your wedding, too."

I pressed a finger to her beautiful, pouty lips. "My only requirement is that you're standing at the end of the aisle. If you make that happen, I'm a happy man for life." I squeezed her lips into fish lips. "As long as you say 'I do.' "

She laughed as I kissed her puckered lips. "I'll be there. That's a given."

"You better be." I tickled her side and she squirmed, pressing her bottom against me. I grabbed her hips and grinded into her. She turned to catch my eyes, groaned, and licked her lips. "Oh, that's it," I said. "You and that luscious ass have done it now."

She laughed as I rose to my knees between her legs, pushing her short nightie up over her breasts. "There's something about making love in a storm..." she said, reaching inside my boxers and pulling my cock out. "You give the term *lightning rod* a whole new meaning, Mr. Rocha."

Her firm, delicate fingers wrapped around me made me weak. She didn't realize the power she yielded over me with her hands, her mouth, and the holy grail between her legs. She could have me on my knees begging in seconds. She stroked me, setting me on fire, making my balls tighten.

Before I lost all sense—forgot my name—I yanked her panties down and spread her thighs wide apart. She kept herself clean shaven except for a small patch of hair I loved the feel of when I sucked her clit. She was glistening and ready for me. I ran a finger between her open lips, spreading her slick wetness.

Jesus, she was a goddess lying before me and she didn't even realize it. Her eyes half closed, the way she moved as I circled my finger between her folds... a fucking goddess.

And she'd agreed to be my wife. How could it possibly be true?

"What is it?" she asked, opening her eyes, propping herself on her elbows and staring at me. "You look lost."

I shook my head. "No. Not lost. I'm right where I always want to be."

A cunning smile cut across her face, and she grabbed my cock again and led it to her opening. "This is where I always want you to be." She wrapped her legs around me and pulled me into her, thrusting her hips up and forward to take me in with a moan and a sigh. "God, I love the feel of you inside me, Merrick."

Fuck. "When you say things like that... you don't even know what it does to me, Rachael."

I held still and watched her buck her hips underneath me, taking me in and out, pulling and pushing with her hips and thighs. It was the sexiest fucking thing my eyes have ever witnessed.

"In that case," she said, "I should tell you that when you make me come, sometimes I see God and hear angels sing. You fuck me so good, Merrick." She let out this whimper-moan and dug her heels into my ass trying to get me to move, but there was no way in hell I was budging a muscle.

She was so amazing riding me from underneath, talking dirty. I'd never been so hard or big in my life. My skin was about to split. If a ring got me this, I could only imagine our wedding night after we said our vows.

I dipped my head and sucked her bottom lip. "What else?" I asked, eager to hear more of her dirty pleasures.

She dug her nails into my ass, making me thrust forward, grinning like the devil. I dove down and bit her nipple, tugging on it until she gasped. "I like it when you're a little rough," she whispered. "You're so big and strong, and when you take me how you want me, it makes me know I'm yours."

God damn. I gritted my teeth, doing everything I could not to pound my dick into her hard and fast. I wanted to draw this out. I'd never been so turned on in my life. If I gave in to it, it would be over way to soon.

I held myself over her, watching her buck and writhe off the bed to slide up and down my cock. Lightning flashed outside the window; the room went bright. She was dripping wet. Thunder rumbled. She hooked her legs around my hips and pulled herself up, taking me deep into her tight, hot pussy. "I need you so bad." She licked my neck and groaned in frustration. "Fuck me, Merrick. Please."

Jesus, how could I resist this? "Tell me one more thing. One more, baby, and I'll fuck you like I never have before."

She reached between us and hooked her finger around the base of my cock, using it for leverage to push me inside her. I came unglued. "Fucking tell me, Rach. One more thing."

"That time," she said, beginning to pant as she used my dick to pleasure herself, "when we walked in on our friends—after when you had me against the door and you touched me." She took my hand and led my fingers between her ass cheeks. "Here." I watched her face shy with her bold words and admission. "I liked it," she whispered.

I kept my fingers where she put them—where she liked them—and kissed her gently. "Baby, I knew you liked it. The way you reacted told me that. Don't be embarrassed."

I grabbed her and flipped her over. "Now you see God and hear angels sing." I pulled her up on her knees, spreading them apart, and pressed down on her back until her ass was in the air and her chest was on the bed. "Fucking perfect. You better grab that pillow and hold on tight."

Holding back one more minute, I pressed my face between her ass, licking from her clit to the dimple at the base of her tailbone. She made a strangled cry into the pillow; her body shivered in response. I could do that all night, but my dick was throbbing painfully and I had to be inside her.

On my knees behind her, I rubbed her pussy with my cock a few times, getting myself wet and making her squirm. "Please," she said, pushing back against me.

I grabbed her hips and shoved inside her, balls deep. She inhaled sharply, fisting the sheets in her hands. I pressed my thumb between her cheeks and took her hard and fast, unrelenting, pounding her, and she loved it. Our bodies smacked together, the sound of her dripping wetness between us audible as I pulled out and thrust back in. I fucked her up the bed to the headboard. She pressed her palms against it, bracing herself. Both of us grunted on the impact of every thrust. She reared back to meet me, eager for every one.

We wanted to climb into each other's skin. Making love wasn't enough. Fucking wasn't enough. Whatever we were doing was what came next and it wasn't enough. We needed more, the complete and utter taking of the other person. Making them lose control—making ourselves lose control. Hell-bent on oblivion through insane orgasm.

She reached back and grabbed my leg, moaning and panting. "Faster." She was right there, so close to coming, I could taste it in the air.

I rocked in and out of her faster, deeper, harder. She made sounds I'd never heard her make. My core burned and shook. When she came, I would go off like a geyser inside her. I pushed my thumb deeper and she cried out. Her body jerked and quaked. I felt her hot gush around me as her contractions brought me to my own orgasm. She tried to put her knees together, but I held them apart and kept thrusting, my own release rushing to the tip of my cock like a fire hose.

All the air went out of my body. The room went black behind my eyes. Sound faded to silence. I think *I* heard angels singing. There was a bright light—either Heaven or lightning. I was inclined to think it was Heaven.

My body collapsed on top of her. Both of us lay there

unmoving, limp, panting, still quaking and moaning with the aftershocks.

"That was..." Her voice trailed off into the pillow.

I slid my hands under her, cupping her breasts, and kissed the back of her neck. "That was something there's no name for. No words to do it justice."

She sighed contentedly. After a few minutes, her breathing turned deeper and slower and I fell into sleep with her.

Eighteen

Rachael

My mom, Aunt Jan, and Maddie stood at the bottom of the grand, curved staircase in the entryway of the hotel. I peeked down at them before descending in my grandmother's wedding dress, which Mom had brought with them.

The vintage white gown fit perfectly. It had off-the-shoulder sleeves that hung to the elbows in gathers of lace and a rounded neckline beaded with a row of pearls. The back plunged in a V to the banded waist. The skirt hung much like the sleeves, in delicate folds of lace. The long train was also made of hand-sewn lace and beaded with a wrist loop underneath for carrying it off the ground at the reception.

I was in love with this dress and never wanted to take it off.

"Merrick's not around, right?" I called down.

"He's outside with MJ and Mr. Simcoe. Do you have it on?" Mom asked, craning her neck to see up to the landing where I stood. "Need help with the buttons?"

"I managed to get them all." The small pearl buttons

were insanely hard to fasten. It took me forever, but I got every one of them.

"Get down here!" Maddie yelled. "We're dying to see you in it."

Stepping carefully down to the first step, I glanced back to make sure the train was straight. I couldn't believe I was standing at the top of the staircase at Turtle Tear in a wedding dress, preparing to become Mrs. Merrick Rocha. It was surreal. Not even a year ago I was interviewing with him for the project manager position to restore the hotel. Now he was mine.

I was afraid I'd wake up and find it was all a dream.

I held on to the railing and took deliberate steps down the staircase. My mom covered her gaping mouth with her hands. Aunt Jan beamed. Maddie grinned. I couldn't suppress the nervous laugh that bubbled out of me. "You like it?"

Mom rushed to me and took my hands. "You're a breathtaking bride."

"Merrick will be blown away," Maddie said, shaking her head in disbelief. "You look like a model out of a bridal magazine."

"That boy won't know what to do with himself." Aunt Jan leaned on the railing. "I just hope he makes it until the wedding night."

Mom shot her a stern look. "Don't dirty up this moment."

MJ jogged into the entryway from the hall. "Don't mind me. I'm just getting the—" His dark eyes, so much like Merrick's, went wide. "Whoa. Rachael. My dad's going to freak when he sees you walking down the aisle."

"Isn't he?" Maddie said, exchanging an awed glance with him.

MJ kept his eyes on her, his expression turning to a smile that dented his Rocha dimples. I knew they were both thinking of the wedding somewhere in their own future.

"Maddie, you'll be a bridesmaid, won't you?" I asked. "And maybe we can sneak you into some bridal gowns, too, while we're finding a dress. You know, just for fun."

Her eyes never left MJ's as she grinned. "I'd love to."

He shook his head, snapping himself out of his fantasy, and pointed to the kitchen. "I was getting drinks." He took a few steps and looked back at Maddie before striding into the kitchen.

"Be right back," she said, and went after him.

"I'm not sure who has it worse," Aunt Jan said. "You or her. Those Rocha men have you both panting after them."

"Hey, I'm not panting," I said, trying not to think of last night and blush furiously in front of my mother.

"What kind of flowers are you thinking of?" Mom asked, ignoring us.

"Yellow calla lilies." It was the first flower Merrick ever gave me and no other would be right to carry.

"With dark green ferns," she said, fussing with my dress. "Oh, it will be so pretty!"

"And not even two months away," Aunt Jan said, eyeing my stomach. "Any reason for the rush?"

I shoved her shoulder. "No. I just wanted to get married around Thanksgiving and there's no reason to wait. We have the location. I have a dress. Why wait?"

"Okay. If you say so." She patted my stomach.

"Don't even joke about that," Mom said, smacking her hand away. "I want to be a grandma, but not yet."

These two would be the death of me. "Nobody's going to be a grandma. I'm going to go take this off and hang it up."

I spun on the stairs and climbed up to the landing thinking maybe a trip to Vegas and a drive-thru Elvis wedding would be a better option.

"Come on. I want to see it," Merrick pleaded, splashing me. We were spending the afternoon at the pool. My mom was reading a trashy romance novel in a lounge chair and Aunt Jan was snoring in hers. Maddie and MJ had disappeared. Mr. Simcoe was pulling weeds from a flower bed, never content to be idle and relax.

"You can't see it until the wedding." I splashed him back, holding on to the side in the deep end with one hand so I didn't go underwater.

He was perched on the side, dangling his legs in the water. "No. I can't see you *in it* until the wedding. I can see the dress."

I laughed. "I'm pretty sure that's not how it goes, but I'll make you a deal."

He shrugged his eyebrows up and down. "Am I going to like this deal?"

"I know I will." I swam between his legs and wrapped my arms around his calves. "I'll show you a picture of it if you make me key lime pie."

He rolled his eyes and groaned, teasing. "You and that sweet tooth of yours."

"You like it as much as I do!"

He lifted and lowered his legs, propelling me forward and back through the water. "Fine. I'll make it. When do I get to see this picture?"

I gave him a shrewd smirk. "As soon as you deliver my pie."

"I'll deliver your pie," he muttered, sliding down into the water and grabbing me between my legs. I let out a startled, high-pitched yelp, making my mom look up from her book.

"Stop," I whispered between clenched teeth, smiling at my mom, hoping she didn't see what he'd just done.

"We live here together. Do you think she doesn't know we sleep together?"

"It's not the sleeping I'm worried about."

Merrick took a deep breath and disappeared under the surface. I watched him sink, then reach out and hook his arms around my legs. I started laughing and kicking, flailing my arms through the water to stay afloat. It was no use. I held my breath just as he tugged me under.

His lips crashed into mine. Our eyes were open and his hands groped me. I play-kicked him and tried to swim away, but he grabbed my foot. We both surfaced, me sputtering and him laughing.

"That's it. No deal." I coughed and made my way to the side. He trapped me between his arms.

"That's too bad. I was going to make two." He grabbed me around the waist and hoisted me up onto the side before hopping up beside me.

"Merrick! Dad!" MJ came running into the pool courtyard, Maddie on his heels. "There's a boat pulling up with a motorcycle on it." He grimaced. "And Nadia."

Merrick lunged to his feet. "Nadia? She's here?"

"Yeah, and some guy," MJ said, shrugging. "They're probably at the dock by now."

"Let's get down there." Merrick reached a hand out to me. I hesitated, but only for a second, before reaching up and taking it.

Nadia at Turtle Tear for an undetermined amount of time—for an undetermined reason. She was Merrick's daughter and she was welcome.

But I didn't have to like it.

The four of us piled into a golf cart and MJ sped off down the path toward the boathouse. I absolutely could not believe she'd shown up. What were the chances?

Merrick's knee bobbed up and down. Nervous. Anxious. That made two of us. A very small part of me was happy for him. I wished it was a larger part of me. There was too much suspicion left inside me from when Nadia showed up at the hotel the first time after sneaking around undetected for a week spying for Enzo. Now she suddenly wanted to change her allegiance? Merrick might be able to take her loyalty at face value, but I need proof and time to accept it.

The boathouse came into view, white with black shutters like the hotel. The long dock jutted out into the water. A square, ferry-like boat was pulled up against it; a side panel opened and lowered onto the dock to unload the motorcycle.

And there she was, black hair blowing in the wind, standing on the dock beside Paul Renault, arm hooked through his. "Looks like you have competition for her affection already," I said, glancing at Merrick.

He didn't respond, only kept his eyes focused on his daughter with a serious expression on his face. I couldn't tell what he was thinking, and that was rare. It was almost like he was searching for signs of himself in her stance, the way she moved. With MJ, the similarity was astounding. With feminine, flirty Nadia, it wasn't as easy other than those damn dimples and her coloring.

MJ stopped the cart and we all got out. I hung back beside Maddie while Merrick and MJ took the lead toward the dock. Nadia, all smiles, waved and came running toward her dad and brother. Merrick's tense shoulders relaxed and his stride quickened. He wanted this and I wanted it for him. I had to.

MJ glanced over his shoulder and gave Maddie and me a leery look. Maddie smiled, encouraging him. She was a better woman that I was. If Nadia had tried to keep Merrick and me apart like she had MJ and Maddie in the past, I would be nowhere on this island with her.

"Dad!" Nadia ran into Merrick's arms and he hugged her tight.

A lump formed in my throat. I equally loved and hated the sight.

"I didn't think I'd see you," he said, holding her back by her shoulders. "Why didn't you call?"

She shrugged as if the stress and heartache she'd given him was no big deal. "When I didn't make it in time to meet you, I figured I'd make it a surprise. Surprise!" She giggled, her best daddy's girl giggle, and tilted her head, blinking innocent eyes.

"And Paul came with you," Merrick said, stepping forward and holding out a hand to shake Paul's. "Good to see you."

"Good to see you," Paul said. He gestured behind them to the bike that the boat driver was unloading. "Papa's bike for you."

"When I arranged to have it shipped, this wasn't what I had in mind, but this is wonderful. Thank you for bringing it." He put a hand on Nadia's back. "And my daughter."

Paul nodded, smiling. "You're welcome."

I stepped up beside Merrick, my stomach sick with nerves. "Hi, Nadia. It's good to see you again." I reached out to hug her as she held her hand out to me. We laughed awkwardly and hugged. I moved on to Paul as MJ stepped up to greet Nadia.

"Welcome," I said to him, "I hope you had a good trip here."

He was all eyes on Nadia, giving me only short glances. *"Très bien,"* he said. "Very nice."

The boy was love struck. Was there a man on earth who Nadia couldn't have under her thumb?

Once all of the introductions were made, MJ and Maddie stowed Paul and Nadia's bags in the golf cart and the four of them headed to the hotel. Merrick saw to tipping the boat driver and ogling over his new bike gleaming in the afternoon sun. He pushed it off the dock into the grass and straddled it. "Want a ride?" he asked, licking his lips and flashing me a sultry smile.

My irresistible man with vibrating steel between his legs. "Oh, I want to ride you." I ran a hand up his leg and squeezed his bulge through his still-damp swim trunks.

He chuckled deep in his throat. "Mama can't resist, huh?"

Mama? Where did this come from?

I told myself I was being ridiculous. He was joking around. Didn't mean anything by it. I mean, sure, I would be Nadia and MJ's stepmom, but I was only a handful of years older than them.

Just. Calm. Down.

"You're a hard man to resist." I hopped on the back and he fired up the engine.

He went slow, navigating the path, avoiding tree roots and ruts that went unnoticed in golf carts. The breeze blew through my wet hair, bringing chills to my skin under the shade of the trees.

"Let's take the long way around!" he shouted over his shoulder to me.

Before I knew it, he was gunning the engine and we were flying through a wide-open expanse of sea grass near the gazebo on the southwest side of the island. I held on tight around his waist, pressing my thighs against his hips. His skin smelled like coconut tanning lotion and chlorine. I placed a kiss between his shoulder blades, wishing we were on the island alone. I'd felt such a disconnect lately, and other than the time we spent in bed trying to drive away the demons that kept causing trouble between us, we hadn't spent real quality time together in weeks.

I wanted my Merrick all to myself. That might never happen again.

Nineteen

Merrick

I saw the subtle yet unmistakable look of words unspoken but understood pass between Rachael and her mom when I introduced Nadia to my future mother-in-law. I had no idea what Rachael had told Sylvia about my daughter, but whatever it was, it wasn't good.

How could I blame Rachael? When she first met Nadia, it was here on the island and Nadia had been a disruptive force sent to do Enzo's dirty work. But what about second chances? If I could welcome my daughter into my life—and how could I not?—couldn't Rachael be a little more willing to give her the benefit of the doubt?

All I wanted was the chance to bring my family together.

Rachael didn't trust easily—I knew that firsthand—but when earned, her loyalty was beyond measure. *I* had to trust that she and Nadia would reach that point.

"How do you all look so much alike?" Jan asked, studying me, MJ, and Nadia from her poolside chaise. "I mean, I get it. He's your dad, but you're like clones!" She laughed. "It's unnatural!"

"Non," Paul said, swinging Nadia's hand tucked in his. "She's prettier."

Rachael glanced up at me, waiting for some fatherly reaction. I didn't have one. Maybe one day I would, but today wasn't that day. I liked Paul and had zero experience being a father to Nadia.

"That's sweet," Rachael said, and I could tell she said it because someone should say something.

"Nadia," Sylvia said, looking up to where we all stood and shading her eyes from her chair below, "did Merrick and Rachael tell you their news?"

We hadn't. There hadn't been time yet. Guess now was that time.

Nadia turned to me, her big, brown eyes round and curious. "What news?"

I took Rachael's left hand and lifted it up for Nadia to see the ring. "We're getting married."

"That's wonderful!" Nadia grabbed Rachael's hand and admired the ring. "Did you set a date?"

"The Saturday after Thanksgiving," Rachael said.

"Wow!" Nadia dropped Rachael's hand. "That's only like six weeks away."

I caught Nadia's eyes darting to Rachael's stomach and somehow I hadn't anticipated that reaction from anyone, but of course people would think she was pregnant.

"No," I said, shaking my head. "It's not for any other reason than that was the date Rachael picked. We're not in a rush because of..." I gestured to Rachael's middle. "Anything else."

I wasn't sure why, but Rachael's eyes narrowed and her lips pursed like she was pissed. Then she pushed her shoulders back and the look was gone. Somehow, my explanation hadn't sat well with her.

What else was new? I was stepping in it at every turn these days. Navigating between these two women was going to be impossible.

"Do you have a dress yet?" Nadia asked Rachael.

"Actually, I do. My mom brought it with her. It was my grandmother's."

There was a pause during which I was sure Rachael was going to offer to show her dress to Nadia, but she didn't. "Why don't we all go back to the hotel," I suggested, "get some drinks, freshen up, and I'll cook tonight. Rach, you can show Nadia your dress."

Nadia clapped her hands together. "Oh, I'd love to see it!"

MJ and Maddie were already heading to the cloister around the courtyard. "I'll get the grill ready," MJ called back to me. Even he had been standoffish toward his sister.

There had to be a way to bring us all together as a family with Nadia included.

I reached out a hand to help Sylvia out of her chaise. "It's your lucky day," I said. "I owe Rachael key lime pie for dessert."

"Thank you," she said, taking my hand and standing. "Are we talking about the famous Turtle Tear key lime pie?"

"That exact one."

"A bride who eats pie six weeks from her wedding?" Nadia said, laughing. "You're brave! Hope that dress has an empire waist."

Rachael tensed. "Out of everything I'm concerned about surrounding this wedding, pie is the least of them."

Jan swung an arm around Rachael's shoulders and started walking toward the cloister. "Wedding planning can be stressful. Just have fun with it." I was thankful Jan was there to diffuse the situation. God knew I'd just make it worse if I opened my mouth.

Sylvia grabbed her bag stuffed with books, sunscreen, and other pool necessities and jogged to catch up with them, leaving me with Paul and Nadia.

"Beautiful place," Paul said.

"Thanks." I ushered them along behind the others. Nadia began speaking to Paul in French and my insides froze. Why it hadn't occurred to me that she would speak to him in his language was beyond me, but the fact that she was telling him things I didn't understand made me nervous. I told myself I would trust her, but I needed transparency to do it. Without it, my mind would run in circles out of my control wondering if she and Paul were sent here by my father.

It was the paranoia of a man who'd been lied to and

manipulated his entire life. Identifying it for what it was didn't stop it, but I wouldn't let it stand between me and my daughter. I was stronger than that.

"That's not how you do it," Sylvia said, monitoring my baking skills. "You should sift your dry ingredients into one bowl and mix the wet in another."

Nadia was upstairs with Maddie checking out Rachael's dress. MJ had taken steaks out to the grill with Paul and Mr. Simcoe, who'd been catching a few z's when we came back to the hotel. I was dying to make my escape out there with them.

"Why don't we take over in here?" Jan said, pouring another glass of wine. "Grilling is a man's job." She made a caveman grunt and laughed. "Get out there with your men and cook the meat."

"Good idea," I said, handing over the mixing spoon to Sylvia. "I'm—"

Rachael started yelling upstairs. The three of us turned in the direction of the entryway, listening, but I couldn't make out her words. "What's she..."

Sylvia shook her head. Jan slugged back her wine. Maddie came running into the kitchen. "Quick!" she said, panicked. "I need seltzer water and a clean towel!"

I darted to the refrigerator. "I've got the seltzer. Towels are in the drawer beside the stove. What happened?"

"Nadia, uh, *spilled* her red wine on Rachael's dress."

Maddie yanked a towel out of the drawer and slammed it shut.

Sylvia gasped and threw her hands up over her lips.

"No," Jan said, setting her glass down on the counter with more force than was normal.

Fuck. Just what I needed. All the women pissed at Nadia. "We'll get it out."

"Wine stains," Jan said, shaking her head.

"We'll fix it," I said. "Accidents happen."

Maddie snorted, grabbing the bottle of seltzer out of my hand and running out of the kitchen. Was she insinuating it wasn't an accident?

"We better go up and see what we can do," Sylvia said. She and Jan walked out of the kitchen like they were on their way to a funeral.

It was a dress. Yes, it had sentimental value, but nobody died. Why did women have to be so dramatic?

I picked up the mixing spoon, figuring I'd better keep up my end of the bargain and make Rachael pie. A minute later, Nadia came in looking like a beaten dog with her tail between her legs.

"She hates me," she said, leaning against the island and setting down her empty wineglass.

"She doesn't hate you," I said, even though I wasn't sure it was true.

"She doesn't think it was an accident." She looked like she was about to cry.

"I'm sure she's just upset. Everything will be fine in

another twenty minutes. Trust me." I grabbed a teaspoon from the drawer beside me and scooped up some key lime filling. "Taste this and tell me what you think."

Her face softened a little as she brought the spoon to her mouth. "Mmm. That's good!"

"Your old man can cook," I said, joking, but the ease of calling myself her old man lit a reassurance in her eyes that I felt inside, too. We'd be okay as long as we stick together. We'd figure this out.

"I won't argue with that," she said, scooping a little more out of the bowl. "How's the Weston Plantation coming along for MJ? I haven't had a chance to talk to him about it."

MJ and I needed to talk. I wanted him to try to have a relationship with his sister. "It's coming along great. They're pretty much done with the house and moving on to the outbuildings. He's had a landscaper in and they've been working since summer on the hundred and fifty acres."

"What's he planning on doing with it?" She picked up the recipe card and started taking over. I wasn't about to stop her.

"Nothing. He and Maddie are going to live there."

"That's it?" She concentrated on transferring the crust mixture into the pie pan. "Seems like a waste." She glanced up at me and shrugged. "You and Rachael live here, but run it as a resort, right? Seems shortsighted to not do anything with that big plantation house with all the space and outbuildings."

My business sense perked up. "What would you do with it?"

A shy smile curved her lips. "Golf course. I'd make one of the outbuildings into a clubhouse with a bar. The other buildings could be rented for meetings or parties."

It was brilliant. Simple and would work perfectly on the property. "We need to discuss your idea with your brother. It has a lot of merit."

"My mom thought so, too." Nadia popped the pan with the crust into the oven. "She's a businesswoman, you know? Well, I guess you probably didn't know."

Considering I thought she'd been dead for the past twenty years, no, I didn't know.

"She owns two car dealerships in Spain." She crossed her arms and smiled at him. "Guess I got the family entrepreneurial genes, huh?"

"That's what you want to do? Own a business?" Finally, something I could help her with.

"More than anything. I hope MJ doesn't pass up the opportunity he's sitting on. I'd love to see him bring out the potential in that property."

A brother-and-sister-owned business? If we talked to MJ, he'd have to see the value in her plan. This could be just what they needed to grow closer. "We'll have to pass your idea by him and see what he thinks."

"Really? You'd talk to him for me?"

I thought we'd do it together, but I didn't want to

disrupt the excitement and happiness I'd given her. "Of course!"

She hurried around the island with her arms open wide. "Thank you, Daddy!" Her embrace paired with calling me Daddy was enough to bolster my confidence one hundred percent.

Everything would turn out fine.

Twenty

Rachael

My grandmother's dress was ruined, and it had been *no* accident. I'd never seen someone fake tripping so poorly in my life. It was like she wanted me to know she was pretending. And she didn't even apologize! How much more obvious could she be?

And I thought Joan was bad with her sarcasm and bitchiness. I'd take a million Joans over one Nadia any day.

Merrick's eyes were on me like a steel trap, like he was waiting for his ticking-time-bomb-of-a-fiancée to explode.

Nadia sat across from him, eating her steak as happy as could be with Paul beside her whispering French love sonnets or something in her ear. I had liked Paul in France, but now that he was with Nadia, I was sour on him, too.

"Nadia made the pie," Merrick said to me, putting a hand on my thigh.

What did he expect me to say? That her pie would make up for everything? I couldn't wear pie down the aisle.

When I didn't respond, he sighed and removed his hand from my leg. Didn't he see what her being here was doing to us? MJ and Maddie were shoveling food in as fast as they could, having made the excuse that MJ had an exam to study for and they had to get back to the Weston Plantation tonight. They'd originally planned to stay for the weekend.

My mom and Aunt Jan sat on the end of the table beside me, staring daggers at Nadia. They were like my own elite force, my first line of defense. You could feel the divide across the table vibrating in the air. I felt terrible for Merrick, but what had been started couldn't just be flipped off like a switch.

He turned to me and brushed my hair back before leaning in to my ear. "It was an accident," he whispered. "Can we get past this, please?"

But it wasn't an accident. He'd never believe that, though. He'd have to find out on his own. "I'd like some of Nadia's pie, please," I said, smiling at her. "I'm sure it's delicious."

Merrick passed me a plate and the pie. I cut myself a big piece and hoped she hadn't poisoned it. I wouldn't put it past her. She was up to something, but I wasn't sure what.

MJ and Maddie stood up from the table. "Thanks for dinner. We have to get back. Mind if we take a boat to the mainland?"

Merrick pushed his chair back. "No, that's fine. I was hoping to talk to you about something, though."

"What's that?" MJ asked, leaning his hands on the back of his chair.

"Well," Merrick said, tossing his napkin on the table and standing up. "Nadia and I were talking earlier and she had a great idea for a business at the Weston Plantation."

And there it was. Nadia's motivation for coming to Turtle Tear. For forging a relationship with her dad. She wanted what he'd given MJ. She wanted her piece of the pie.

I wanted to throw the whole pie in her face and had to keep myself from doing just that.

"We're not opening a business," MJ said, crossing his arms. Maddie glared at Nadia. "We're keeping it as our home," he said.

"I know. I know." Merrick rounded the table. "It's a good idea, though, and wouldn't interfere with the main house, so I thought I'd run it by you, that's all."

Maddie gave me a look that said if I was planning to tie cement blocks to Nadia's feet tonight and toss her in the water and leave her as gator food, I could count her in. Mr. Simcoe watched the exchange with growing curiosity. I could see the wheels in his head turning. I wondered if he would say anything to Merrick about it. Merrick had grown to take Mr. Simcoe's wise advice as gospel.

Nadia watched her dad and brother with a blank expression. Too blank, like a chameleon trying to figure out which color to turn. MJ was an uncertainty to her. He wielded as much power over Merrick as she did—more, truth be told, although Merrick might tell himself otherwise.

Merrick clapped a hand on MJ's shoulder. "Come on. I'll drive you two over in the boat and we'll talk on the way." He turned to look back over his shoulder. "Be back in a bit," he said to me.

It was happening already—I was fading into the background. No kiss good-bye. No invitation to ride along, just a fleeting thought and a toss of *be back in a bit* over his shoulder.

This girl had to get off my island.

Later that night, Mom, Aunt Jan, Mr. Simcoe, and I sat at a table in the lounge playing gin rummy while Merrick and Nadia chatted by the fireplace. Paul had gone to bed, exhausted from the time change from France to Florida.

I was losing by a landslide, too focused on what Merrick was talking about to pay attention to the game.

"If you make it private," he said, "you have dues to sustain the day-to-day operations, and special events are just gravy."

"True," Nadia said, "but it's difficult to bring in new members without an established word-of-mouth recommendation."

Merrick nodded. "I see your point."

To me, her point didn't matter. MJ and Maddie didn't want to turn their backyard into a business. I knew what he was thinking: A family business would bring them all together. But he was wrong. It wouldn't. I couldn't sit there any longer and listen without saying something.

"I'm out," I said, laying my cards on the table. "I can barely keep my eyes open."

After kissing each of them on the cheek, I eased over to where Merrick sat. He took my hand and looked up at me. "I'm going to bed," I said. "Come up with me?"

He looked from me to Nadia and back. "In a bit."

I bent down so I was level with his ear. "I think you should come up now. I want to talk with you privately."

Nadia stared into the fire, looking like she'd just lost her puppy. She knew how to play him; that was for sure. "Give me twenty minutes and I'll be up." He pressed a quick kiss to my lips before turning back to her, dismissing me.

I reined in my annoyance and strode down the hallway. I'd give him twenty minutes and then come back down and drag him up by his hair. I understood this was his daughter and he was bonding with her, but he was also setting a dangerous precedent for me. I wouldn't be pushed to the side for Nadia for the rest of my life.

Up in our bedroom, I sat on the bed and watched the clock. It was the longest eighteen minutes of my life before the door opened and he came in. He saw me sitting there and stopped. "What are you doing?"

"Waiting for you." I had to play this cool if I wanted to get anywhere other than another argument. I held my hand out for him to come to me.

Merrick sat beside me, gathered me in his arms, and pulled me up the bed until we were lying with my head on his chest. "That's better," he said. "Are you having a good visit with your mom and Aunt Jan?"

I pressed my palm to his chest, splaying my fingers. I soaked him in, his heat, his heartbeat, the aura he let off that was all Merrick. He calmed me. "Yeah, I'm glad they came."

"Nadia feels terrible about your dress." His chin dipped as he looked down at me.

I couldn't look him in the eye. "She does?"

"Well, of course. I'm sure she told you."

"No. She didn't." I closed my eyes, waiting for him to respond. It took a moment.

"I'm sure she was just embarrassed and wanted to forget about it."

Oh yeah, that was it. "So what's the big idea you and Nadia thought up for MJ's property?"

His head nodded even lower, trying to see my face. "Why do you say it like that?" He lifted my chin so I had to look at him.

"Like what?"

"Like I'm planning some hostile takeover of the Weston Plantation."

I shot up on my hands, holding myself over him. "Why are you getting so defensive? I only asked what you two have been talking about all night."

"I'm defensive? You're the one all put out because I spent an evening talking with my daughter." He pulled me back down onto his chest. "Stop, Rachael. Please. I need this to work."

I blinked away the tears in my eyes. "I know." I couldn't see how it could work.

The next morning I woke alone. I found Paul out on the patio drinking coffee. "Morning," I said, sitting down in the chair next to him.

"Good morning. Merrick and Nadia took the bike out." He pointed into the distance beyond the pool cloister.

"Oh. Okay." I knew my mom and Aunt Jan liked to go for morning walks before it got too hot out. "Looks like it's just us then. Would you like some breakfast?"

"*Non.* Coffee's fine." He smiled and I caught a glimpse of Mama Renault in his expression.

"It's a shame your mom and dad couldn't come over with you. I enjoyed meeting them."

"They don't travel. Papa says he's too old."

"You and Nadia seem to be getting along well." I managed to smile.

"She's a lovely girl. Nice family." He reached over and patted my hand. He had no idea. Her family was wound tightly in a web of deceit, and that was what she grew up knowing. Nadia was lovely outside, but inside...

"How long will you be staying with us?" Possibly his answer would give me insight into Nadia's plans.

"Just the weekend."

"It's too bad you can't stay longer. Will Nadia be going back with you, or staying here?" I couldn't help the anxious hope that she would be leaving.

Paul's forehead creased in confusion. "She said she was moving here to live."

My stomach rolled. That was what I was afraid of. "Oh. Right. I'm sure Merrick knows. I wasn't sure she had decided yet."

His face eased back into a smile. "I'll miss her."

"You're welcome to come visit anytime." Or better yet, he could take her back to France for the rest of her life.

The Harley's engine rumbled toward us from far out. I shaded my eyes and watched, waiting for them to come into view. When they rounded the corner of the pool cloister, my heart lightened at the sight of Merrick's smile—bigger than I'd seen it in weeks—and Nadia laughing, hanging on to her dad for dear life.

I found myself laughing, too, as they approached, instantly regretting having hard feelings toward Nadia. Maybe spilling her wine on my dress had been an accident she was ashamed of and eager to forget, even if it hadn't looked that way. If it wasn't, maybe she held animosity toward me for being close to the man she'd never gotten the chance to know.

I shouldn't be so unforgiving. I had to try. For Merrick. For all of us.

They stopped just outside the patio gate and Merrick turned off the engine. "Looks like you guys were having fun!" I called.

Nadia flung her hair back over her shoulders, flushed and exhilarated. "That was awesome."

She came through the gate and sat right down on Paul's lap.

Merrick ran his fingers through his windblown hair and sauntered over to the table. "Good morning," he said, bending to kiss me.

He pulled a chair out and sat down, stretching his arms over his head. "That's the way to start a day."

"I know, right?" Nadia said, bubbling over from his attention.

"I was thinking," I said, eager to jump into the moment with both feet, "maybe you'd want to go to the mainland with me today to look at dresses?"

Her face fell. Merrick coughed and looked down at the ground. "I'm so sorry for ruining your dress," she said. "The stain won't come out?"

My intention of joining in their good times had the opposite effect and killed the mood. "It might yet. I just thought it would be fun to get out and see what the options were. Try some things on. What do you think?"

"Um. Okay. As long as we're not gone too long. Paul leaves tomorrow afternoon. I want to spend as much time with him as I can." She pressed a kiss to Paul's cheek.

"Why don't we come, too?" Merrick asked. "Paul and I can check out that sixty-inch TV I've had my eye on for the apartment in Atlanta while you ladies do your dress shopping."

"That's perfect!" Nadia said, bouncing on Paul's lap.

The afternoon found Nadia and me in a small boutique with pink floral Victorian love seats and black-curtained dressing rooms. I stood on a carpeted riser in front of a gilded, fairy-princess-style mirror in an enormous, beaded monstrosity of a dress with more tulle than I ever imagined could be sewn on one garment. The lace and sequin train was entwined with gold velvet roping.

Nadia picked it out.

It was revolting.

"You look like a queen!" she said from where she perched on one of the love seats. "It's perfect. My dad will die when he sees you in this!"

Yes, he would. Merrick would die of laughter if he saw me in this dress. "I don't know," I said, trying to spin around enough to look at the back. "It's not really me."

"Well, maybe you need to be less you and more what he needs you to be."

Whoa. I couldn't have heard her correctly. "Excuse me?"

She swiveled in her seat, trying to look uncomfortable with this discussion, but she couldn't hide the spark of fire in her eyes from the pending confrontation.

I'd had her pegged correctly all along.

"I just mean, he's a pretty big deal even if Rocha Enterprises is...well, after talking to him last night, I would say the company is only on hiatus. He's done business all over the world. Did you know he designed a high-rise for a prince in Dubai?" She clasped her hands on her lap and let her head tilt innocently. "I'm just saying, if you love him, you'll push him. He needs someone to get him back up on that horse, Rachael, and I'm sorry, but from where I'm sitting, it looks like you're content to let him lounge around on that island and waste his life."

"Waste his life!" My head was on fire from the explosion going off in my brain. "How dare you say his life with me is a waste! You've been with him all of a day and you think you know what's best for him?"

The bridal consultant started to enter the room and backed out again. Nadia, clearly pleased that she'd gotten under my skin, feigned composure. "When was the last time you talked to him about his dreams? About what he wants for the future other than getting married? Didn't you see how alive he was last night talking about a potential project at the Weston Plantation? How animated he was? Why aren't you encouraging him?"

"Why are you? So he can build up a mass of properties and Enzo can try to take them from him again? Or will it be you this time who stabs him in the back? Again?" I stepped down from the platform and took a few steps toward her, failing to look as intimidating in the mountain of tulle as I'd hoped. "Don't judge me when you've been on the side inflicting pain all of this time. I've been here helping him pick up what's left and move on. Now you stride into our lives with God knows what ulterior motive—although I have my suspicions—and start telling me how I'm failing him? No way. I won't stand here and listen to this."

"What suspicions, Rachael?" she asked, calmly picking her nail.

"Just be warned. I won't let you manipulate him." I hefted up the ten pounds of skirting and stormed into the dressing room. I was shaking I was so mad. How dare she insinuate that I'm not good for Merrick. That she somehow knows his needs better than I do.

I reached behind me for the zipper to the god-awful ugly dress I'd indulged her in trying on, only to find I couldn't reach it and needed the consultant's help. If I didn't get my temper under control, I'd be tearing the thing off by the seams in seconds.

Sticking my head out through the curtain, I choked at the sight in front of my eyes. Nadia was crying in Merrick's arms with Paul patting her back. I was the big bad stepmom already and hadn't even made it down the aisle. Merrick's eyes found me, hard and ringed in disbelief. How could I do this to him? That was the question I was certain we were both asking ourselves, but only I knew I was justified. I wouldn't stand by and let anyone verbally attack me, even his precious Nadia.

Merrick eased her out of his arms into Paul's and strode toward me with a lethal look that made my stomach flutter. I stepped backward farther into the dressing room and he followed me in, shaking his head. "Why?" he asked, setting his hands on his hips.

"Did you ask *her* why?"

He threw out a hand. "She won't stop crying long enough to talk about it! What did you say to her?"

"What did *I* say to *her*? How about what did *she* say to me, Merrick?" I spun around, fidgeting in the dress, trying to unwrap it from around my legs. "Please unzip me!"

He did and I let the dress fall off my shoulders, thankful to be out of the heavy, hot material. "Well?" he said, turning me around by the shoulders.

I took the opportunity to balance and step out of the skirt and slip. "She told me I wasn't good for you. What was I supposed to do? Agree with her?"

He squeezed my shoulders, pulling me upright to stand straight in front of him. "I doubt very much that's what she meant. Her meaning was probably lost in the interpretation."

"Interpretation? So now I'm stupid and didn't hear what I heard?" I shoved his hands off me. "You have to be kidding me."

He shoved his fingers through his hair like he always did when he was frustrated, making it puffy on top. I would've laughed if I wasn't about to cry. "I'm not saying you didn't hear whatever you heard. I'm just saying she probably didn't mean it like it sounded. Sometimes things come out wrong."

"This is a very one-sided conversation. Unless you care to take what I have to say seriously, then there's no reason to talk about it anymore."

Merrick turned and let his forehead fall against the wall. "Jesus, Rachael. Why can't you just get along with her?"

"Why can't I... Why do you assume it's me that can't get along with her? Everything was going swimmingly until she told me I basically suck ass at being your girlfriend and had to step it up if I deserved to marry you."

He turned his head and raised his eyebrows in condescension. "Seriously? That's what she said?"

I gritted my teeth and squeezed my hands into fists at my sides. "You better get that fucking look off your face right now, Merrick Rocha, if you know what's good for you."

He laughed. I could not believe he was laughing. "I'm sorry," he said, and waved a hand in the air. "But you trying to be intimidating is just funny."

I let out a frustrated groan and he laughed harder, holding his stomach. "I hate you," I said, and crossed my arms, glaring at him, which he found absolutely hysterical.

Watching him crack up leaning against the wall of the tiny five-foot-by-five-foot dressing room with the hideous dress swaddled around our calves made me start to get giddy. At first, I couldn't stop the smile from spreading on my lips even by biting my cheeks, then I was giggling, and finally full out laughing with him.

"There's something very wrong with you," I told him between fits of laughter.

"It's been a stressful few weeks. I guess I just... snapped." His face was red from laughing and my mascara was running. I could only imagine what Paul, Nadia, and the bridal consultant were thinking. First we're yelling at each other, then the next thing you know, we're laughing like loons.

Merrick reached out and pulled me to him. "Come here. I don't care what anyone says or what you hear or think you hear or didn't hear. Listen to *me*, okay. I love you." He took my face between his hands. "I want to marry you and be with you forever. I know accepting Nadia after everything in my past with her and Enzo and her mother is hard for you. It's not easy for me either, but I want to go forward in a good way and leave all of that behind, especially now that my future looks so beautiful." His eyes dropped to the dress on the floor. "Even beautiful in this terrible dress, but if you like it, who am I to complain?" He winked and kissed me. I ran my hands up his chest and behind his neck, holding him and deepening the kiss.

Even when we fought, we didn't really fight; we just blew off steam and picked up where we left off. But it was like putting a Band-Aid over a gaping wound that needed stitches. It still bled and the Band-Aid would soon fall off and we'd be back where we were—at odds about Nadia.

I knew this in my heart, but when I was held tight in Merrick's arms, it didn't seem to matter.

Twenty-One

Merrick

I was losing my mind. All I could think about was making Rachael forget everything that had happened by shoving her up against the wall, spreading her legs, and proving to her just how much she was mine. I didn't care who was outside that curtain or how much money the dress on the floor was that I was trampling all over.

Never breaking our kiss, I grasped the backs of her thighs and lifted her, turning us so she was against the wall. She pulled her lips away and slid them to my ear. "What are you doing?" she whispered.

"Apologizing." I crushed my lips to hers again, teasing her with my tongue to open her mouth. She did and let out the sweetest moan I'd ever heard. I slipped my fingers inside her damp panties, pushing them aside so I could touch her, get inside her.

Needing me, too, she flicked the button on my pants open and tugged the zipper down. "Hurry," she pleaded, taking me out and positioning me at her entrance. I fell against her, letting my hips guide me up into her wet heat. She dug her fingernails into my shoulders. Her thighs tightened around me. I thrust urgently, desperately. We had to find ourselves again. I was so sick of arguing with her. Making love was our language, not fighting.

She whimpered and shook. I felt her contracting and pulsing around me. It was too much sensation to hold back. I held her tight and let it take me under.

We stood, slack against the wall, breathing each other in, savoring the last seconds of togetherness, when there was a knock against the frame of the curtained room. "Do you need help in there?" a woman asked.

Rachael grimaced and her legs shot down to the floor. "No. I've got it. Thanks."

"Yes, you do," I whispered, nipping her earlobe.

She let out a breathless laugh, tucked me back into my pants, and zipped me up. I cupped her cheek and looked into her eyes. So many words were in there, left unspoken between us. I knew this was only the beginning of our struggles, but God, I loved her and we could make it through. "Get dressed." I kissed her forehead and left the dressing room.

Nadia and Paul were waiting on the sidewalk outside the dress shop. Thankfully, she'd stopped crying and looked like nothing had happened. "We were talking about getting dinner somewhere," she said. "Know any good restaurants around here?"

"There are a few." I pointed up the street to the corner. "Angelo's has great Italian. A little farther up there's Poseidon's Table. Dumb name, amazing seafood." I knew

Rachael had wanted to hit Poseidon's the last time we were in town shopping, but we were meeting Beck back at the boat and ran out of time. The last thing I was going to do, though, was mention how Poseidon's would be Rachael's choice. Too soon. I was avoiding more tears at all costs.

Nadia squeezed Paul's arm and leaned her head against his shoulder. "What do you think?" she asked, gazing up at him.

A protective streak ran through me and I suddenly wanted to threaten him with his life if he hurt her. If I ever saw her cry again, it would be too soon.

Rachael pushed out the door and stepped onto the side-walk, avoiding eye contact with all of us. Awkward tension banded around us and held on tight.

I needed a drink. "Where are we eating, Paul?"

He gazed down at Nadia. "Seafood?"

She shrugged. "If you want."

He smiled and kissed her cheek. "Italian it is."

Rachael sighed. I took her hand and led us down the street to the corner.

Angelo's was a cave of dark red booths, ancient black casino carpeting, a megalith of a mahogany bar that looked more like an altar pillaged from an old Catholic church than a bar, and dim candlelight from stubs in dirty glass holders on each table.

It was a hole, but the lobster ravioli melted in your mouth. Rachael was on her third glass of merlot and I took the last swig of my second Jameson on the rocks, which had smoothed the sharp edge, but in no way eliminated it altogether.

"The Renault Vineyard should distribute to the U.S.," Paul said, swirling his own merlot around in his wineglass. He'd carried the conversation for the past almost hour now and was doing surprisingly well. He spoke better English than he'd let on.

"When you take over, you can make it as big as you want," Nadia said, and tapped him on the nose. For some reason, she turned her eyes on Rachael then. "Paul has big plans for his parents' company when he takes it over in a few years. I think they're brilliant." She snugged against Paul's side. "I can't wait to order Renault wine in every restaurant in the world!"

Rachael stabbed a ravioli then let her fork drop and kicked back a big gulp of wine. "Full?" I asked her, patting her leg.

"Something like that." She turned to me and her tight expression softened. "I'm just ready to get home. I'm not feeling well."

It had been a long day, and it was not like I'd eased her into a relationship with Nadia. She was stuck on an island with her where there was no buffer. After today and whatever went down between them, it would only be harder to deal with.

The server approached the table. "Anyone save room for dessert?"

"I think we're—"

"Yes," Nadia said when I was hoping to end this dinner

and get Rachael home to the privacy of our tree house. "Chocolate cake and cappuccino."

"Anyone else?" the server asked.

Nadia nudged Paul. *"Non,"* he said, rubbing his stomach. "I'm full."

"Come on," she pleaded. "At least have a cappuccino."

He held up his hands in surrender. "Okay. A cappuccino, please."

"Great." The server turned to Rachael and me. We both shook our heads, no.

We sat for another half hour watching Nadia eat her cake and her and Paul sip their cappuccinos. It was almost physically painful knowing Rachael wanted to bolt for the door and never look back. If she weren't there, it would've been fine. I hated thinking that way, but it was true. I didn't want to live my life divided between Rachael and Nadia, but the odds of them getting along were looking slim. That left one option: letting one of them go.

That couldn't happen either, so I was effectively fucked by these two stubborn women.

Rachael and I soaked in the sunken hot tub in the tree house. Never one to hold much alcohol, she had her eyes closed. I picked up her foot and propped it on my lap, rubbing my thumbs over her instep. We needed to talk, but dredging up the day was the last thing I wanted to do.

This morning when she'd suggested a shopping trip,

she'd been trying so hard to bond with Nadia. Whatever happened between them had to have been a misunderstanding. Rachael would never hurt my daughter intentionally and I couldn't believe Nadia would set out to hurt Rachael either.

"Come here," I said, pulling her calf to get her to cross the hot tub to me.

Her eyes opened and I saw the sorrow in them. We needed to talk about this, but we wouldn't.

I took her onto my lap and held her against me in the bubbling water. I needed to feel her heart beat and touch her soft skin. Without her, I had nothing.

This was just one puzzle piece in the big jigsaw puzzle picture of our lives together that wasn't fitting quite right. But it would. We'd find a way to make it fit.

"You okay?" I asked her, cradling her head against my shoulder.

She shrugged.

"Tomorrow's a fresh start." I tipped her chin up and kissed her hard, intent on conveying my trust in her, my belief that she could overcome this rift between her and Nadia.

Twenty-Two

Rachael

The next morning I got up early. Mom and Mr. Simcoe were talking plants and boring me and Aunt Jan to tears, so we took off for the orchard.

"You have something on your mind, so spill it," Aunt Jan said.

I could never hide anything from her. "Nadia's hell-bent on making me hate her for some reason."

"It's working?" She chuckled.

"Oh yeah. I don't know what to do. Merrick and I fight all the time about her. He's determined to believe she's his little princess even though she's Satan's spawn and she has no intention of leaving anytime soon." I slashed the big stick I was carrying across some tall sea grass. "We got into it yesterday in the dress shop. Next thing I knew, Merrick was there, she's bawling her eyes out in his arms, and I'm the evil stepmom in *Cinderella*."

"That's a tough one." Aunt Jan stopped to watch a heron take off from a tree along the path. "Why do you think she's got it out for you?"

"All I can figure is she doesn't want any competition

for her daddy's affections. She wants him all to herself, so when he kicks off, she gets all his cash. She's consumed with the idea that he'll start up Rocha Enterprises again. She thinks he's wasting his life here doing nothing."

She gave me a sideways glance. "Is he? I mean, if you take an objective look at the situation. You know him better than she does. Should he be retired in his early thirties? Will he be happy doing nothing for the rest of his life?"

"Thanks. You sound just like her." I smacked my stick into the ground.

"Don't get pissy with me. Sometimes we're too close to the trees to see the forest—is that the expression?"

"Something like that."

"I'm not saying she was right and you were wrong. It's not about right and wrong, it's about finding a seed of truth to plant in common ground."

I stopped and stared at her. "Wow, you're all kinds of philosophical this morning."

"No coffee yet. I'm very Zen."

We walked down the rows of fruitless key lime trees. The citrus scent still clung to the leaves and grass. Thinking that maybe there was a seed of truth in Nadia's claim that I wasn't encouraging Merrick like I should be was a bitter pill to choke down, but like Aunt Jan said, I had to consider everything she said objectively.

Maybe she was right.

The problem was, I hadn't known Merrick in his business prime, when everything was going his way and the real estate development industry was bowing at his feet. I came in at the end when his legacy was a minute from being flushed down the drain.

But there was one person who knew the Rocha Enterprises Merrick like the back of her hand.

What was the saying? Keep your friends close, but your enemies closer? Something like that. Like Aunt Jan, I was feeling Zen.

Beck and Joan landed on the island just after noon. I hadn't told Merrick they were coming. "What's this about the dickhead getting a vintage Harley?" Beck asked. "He's not going to kick me off the island for coming to see it, is he?"

I grabbed his arm as the three of us walked toward the golf cart. I'd missed him. "No. He'll probably want to break down and give you a big ol' man hug for being here. His women are ready to kill each other."

"I heard Nadia was here," Joan said. "Things not going well on Paradise Island?"

I laughed and shook my head. "Don't piss me off, Joan. You're the real reason I wanted you guys here. I need to talk to you."

"You want to talk to me?"

"Shit," Beck said. "It must be bad."

"I need your perspective," I told her.

"Well," she said, sitting down in the golf cart, "we've reached a new level of awkward."

Beck got behind the wheel out of habit. "I think it's referred to as friendship."

"No," Joan and I both said in unison, then acknowledged each other with mutual smirks. What we had was the ability to put differences aside for both of our benefit when needed. We had zero in common outside of the people we both cared about. If it weren't for them, we'd never speak again.

"Whatever," Beck said. "I'm glad I had brothers. I don't get you women at all."

"Yeah, yeah," I said, pointing to the left. "Go to the boathouse. We'll leave you there with Merrick and his new toy."

At the boathouse, I put my finger up to my lips to tell them to be quiet as I turned the door handle. Merrick was alone inside, rubbing a soft rag over the Harley's gas tank. "Hey," I said. "I have a surprise."

He walked toward me smiling. "I like your kind of surprises." He snapped the towel, aiming for my hip, but I dodged out of the way.

"Not that kind of surprise." I opened the door wide and Beck stepped in.

"I'm allowed visits still, right?" he said, holding a hand out to Merrick.

Merrick looked like he'd just been thrown a life raft as he shook Beck's hand, then pulled him in for a man-hug-back-pat thing. "Good to see you, man. Glad you came out."

Beck's eyes roamed the Harley and he whistled. "Look at that fucking thing. How'd you get that, you lucky bastard?"

I grabbed Joan's wrist. "Come on. Let's leave them in their shiny metal and motorized glory."

"Okay," she said, letting me lead her away, "but I have a feeling I'm going to need a drink for this convo we're about to have."

Nadia and Paul were spending his last hours at the pool. Mr. Simcoe had taken Mom and Aunt Jan out on the boat for their final afternoon here. Joan and I sat at the kitchen island. I'd made her a strong margarita and nervously munched on chips, unsure how to begin.

Joan tapped her fingernails on the countertop. "You're not going to ask me about sex, are you?"

I dropped a chip onto the floor. "Sex? No. Why would I need to ask you about sex?"

She shrugged. "You know. He and I have a history in that department, so I figured if you were having problems..."

"We're not having problems with sex!" This was a mistake. Too late to turn back now. "Do you think he's happy being retired?"

"Oh," she said, leaning back and staring across the room, considering her answer. "For now I think he is. He was under a tremendous amount of stress for a long time before you came into the picture. He was burnt out. Sick of the politics of the industry. This is a nice break for him."

"But you said break, so you think he'll rebuild Rocha again?"

She nodded enthusiastically. "No question. Merrick has

too much ambition, too much motivation, and too many ideas not to act on them. I give him three years tops. You two will get married. You'll pop out a kid and he'll be ready to have his professional life back."

How did everyone see the future so clearly when all I saw was a blur? How did Nadia and Joan know Merrick so much better than me? I knew he was brilliant and talented and driven, but he'd been so content with letting his company go, like he knew it was time. He turned the page with grace and, as far as I knew, had never suffered doubts.

I wasn't some stupid dreamer who thought that a baby and I would be all he'd need. Joan made perfect sense. He'd want a rounded life with family and a career. Hell, I did, too…I think. We hadn't gotten that far. We knew we wanted to be married and someday we'd probably have a baby, but we were okay with not planning our lives farther than now. Why was everyone else looking ahead for us?

"Was there something else?" Joan asked. The way she watched me, there was no way she couldn't see the turmoil going on inside my head.

I gave in and let out my fear, sat it right between us… with Joan of all people. "I'm afraid I'm not good for him because I haven't even thought about him working again. I haven't asked him or encouraged him. I just took it at face value that he did what made him happy and he seems like he is. Nadia said I wasn't good for him because I wasn't helping him get back up on that horse. I just—"

"Knock it off, Rachael. What's making you act like a

whiny baby? You've always been strong enough to stand up to me and now this chick strolls in and says he's her dad and you're falling apart? Get your shit together, woman."

She leaned her elbows on the island, coming closer to me. "Listen to me. We both know Merrick's not a child. For all intents and purposes, he raised himself and his sister. He knows what he wants and gets it. You don't have to guess or push him. He's not one of those men who need a mommy. He needs a partner and that's what you are to him. So stop questioning everything."

Laughter blurted out of my mouth. Just like I thought, Joan didn't hold back. "Thanks. That was exactly the kick in the ass I needed." I felt better than I had in days.

"I'd let you hug me, but we both know we don't want that." She reached over and grabbed a handful of chips from the bag. "Maddie's been racking her brain trying to think up ways to keep Nadia away from the Weston Plantation. I swear, you two are acting like a tsunami blew in and wrecked your lives." She waved a hand in the air. "Treat her like any other petulant child trying to get attention and *ignore her*. She'll go away."

"Merrick won't ignore her; that's the problem. And she won't ignore me. I think she's trying to come between him and me, so she's up my ass with these comments trying to provoke me so he'll think it's me confronting her instead of the other way around."

She took a sip of her drink. "It's working."

I dropped my forehead against the counter. "I know."

"Ignore. Her."

I raised my head. "It's that easy?"

A sly smile crept across her lips. "It's that easy."

I had my doubts, but what other option did I have?

Twenty-Three

Merrick

Having Beck here made me question asking him to leave in the first place. It was a relief having someone to confide in that was outside of the situation. Plus, it was Beck, and I had to admit I missed the guy.

Having been raised by the duplicitous asshole that was my father, I'd never trusted another man enough to call one a friend. They were peers, employees, or competitors, but definitely never friends.

Beck was the first guy I ever trusted and called friend. Lucky for him, that meant I dumped every last effed-up detail on him. Every last thing that had come up since Nadia called from France.

"This is definitely messed up," he said, leaning against the worktable. I hadn't moved one thing from his desk or touched any of his tools. He'd left most of them behind, like he knew I'd need him to come back.

"As messed up as Rachael and Joan running off together like they did?" Rachael had grabbed Joan's wrist like they were best friends. That was not normal.

Beck dropped his head and looked at me like I was missing something. "Really, dude?" He shifted and crossed his arms. "Let's put it this way. When I was a kid, we had two cats, both female. They hated each other. Never did get used to living together. Then my mom thought she'd bring a third cat home—also female. The first two teamed up against the new one. It's like some kind of crazy woman thing. It's innate in their species. They hate each other until there's a bigger threat, then it's on."

"Ah," I said, getting a clear picture. "Nadia's the bigger threat. I can see why Rachael would feel that way—even if it's not true—but why would Joan?"

Beck waved a finger. "It's not just Joan. Maddie's been having fits, too, ever since catching wind of Nadia having some grand plan for the Weston Plantation. That's stepping into Maddie and Joan's territory."

"Jesus. Navigating around these woman is like walking through a mine field. I didn't feel this pressured when I had to find my way around government regulations in foreign countries. At least then the rules didn't change overnight."

Beck laughed and picked up a wrench, tapping it in the palm of his hand. "You know what you need to do, right? Find something for Nadia that doesn't involve this place or MJ's. Keep her busy somewhere else. Divide these women up."

Divide and conquer. "Good plan. But that means I'll be busting my ass to keep them apart for the rest of my life." No good. "They have to find a way to get along. That's all there is to it."

Beck stretched and came to stand next to me, admiring the bike. "Good luck." He smacked me on the back and chuckled. "For once, I'm glad I'm not you."

I balled up the towel I'd been polishing the Harley with and tossed it on his desk. "So, what about you? How're things at MJ's place? I hear you guys wrapped up the west wing."

"We did. Looks great, too. That place is coming together. He wants to start on the big outbuilding next, make it into a guest house. Joan's got someone working on the plans."

"Why didn't anyone mention this to me? Rachael could draw up those plans, no problem. She'd love it." MJ and I needed to have a little talk.

"Listen, I don't want to get into the middle of all of this, but I think MJ figured it would be easier if he had someone else do it. That way Nadia wouldn't get involved and it wouldn't end up being turned into a country club clubhouse."

"She's his sister. He can't turn his back on her, too. I won't have them all against her when she hasn't done anything—"

"This time." Beck shot me a stern look. "Not everyone can be as forgiving as you. If you push her on them, it'll blow up in your face. Give them time to come around on their own."

Damn, he was right. I wasn't a patient person. Square pegs fit in round holes if you cut the angles off. That's what I did. I made things happen whether they were meant to or not. Sometimes it worked—like with Rachael—and sometimes it didn't, but I always grabbed what I wanted by the neck and didn't let go. "What am I supposed to do in the meantime? Let them plot against each other? Ignore the tears and the arguing?" I paced in a circle, shoving my hands through my hair. "I can't take this, man. I'm on the edge here."

"Yeah, you're stuck." Beck tossed a leg over the bike and sat on the seat. "You don't want Nadia to leave and Rachael lives here. Not that you'd want her to go either. Right?"

"Of course not. They both have to be here. Guess I could build an octagon and let them go at it MMA style."

Beck threw his head back and laughed. "Now you're talking. I put a grand on Joan to whip all their asses."

"Shit. I'm with you on that." I sat down at his desk and kicked my feet up on it. "How's that going anyway? You and Joan?"

He grasped the bike's handles and leaned back. "You know, I've dated competitive women in the past. The difference this time is that she's not competing with me. That's a plus. To be honest, my issue is how everyone else sees her. It's like dating Dracula or something. Everyone thinks she's this horrible monster. Once you get past that tough exterior, though, she's nothing like that."

I knew what he was talking about from past experience. Although Joan and I never got as close personally as we did physically, she let me see past her tough chick routine every once in a while. "Do you like what's in there?"

He laughed. "That sounds dirty."

I chuckled and let it go. Joking was his way of changing the conversation when it came to something he didn't want to talk about. "We should probably go make sure Joan and Rachael haven't tied Nadia to a tree and set it on fire."

"If we must." He got off the bike and we headed for the door.

"Thought about Nebraska?" I asked.

"Thought about it. Haven't gone. Obviously."

"Yeah." There was another square peg I'd shoved into a hole it might not actually fit in anymore. "Well, if you don't want to go back, you can hang around here. Only if it's what you want, though. Don't do it for me."

"Why the hell would I do anything for you, ya selfish bastard?" He patted my shoulder and shook his head, smiling.

The bonfire flames licked the air, crackling and sending smoke up into the sky. Nadia wasn't tied to a post in the center of it, but judging by the looks on Rachael and Joan's faces, she was lucky not to be.

It was a little past seven in the evening and the sun had just set. Paul, Sylvia, and Jan had to be heading out to get to the airport soon, but we thought a quick hot dog roast like Rachael used to have in her backyard when she was little would be fun while her mom and aunt were there.

"Stick a fork in me," Jan said, leaning back in her chair

with a hand on her stomach. “You’re a good weenie roaster, Merrick.”

“Thanks, Jan. Better to be a weenie roaster than a weenie.”

Beside me, Nadia burst out laughing. “That’s hysterical!”

Rachael and Joan exchanged irritated glances. It pissed me off. Nadia wanted my affection. Sure, her fake laughter was pretty obvious, but it didn’t deserve their level of criticism.

I eyed Rachael across the fire. She collected herself and shut off the blatant disregard for Nadia’s feelings. And mine.

What the hell was going to happen when it was only the three of us on this island?

“How long are you staying, Nadia?” Joan asked.

“As long as my dad will let me,” she said, turning to me with what surely passed as puppy dog eyes.

I wasn’t stupid. I knew what she was up to, but still... she was my daughter. Hearing her call me Dad was awesome. “You’re welcome for as long as you’d like to be here.”

She lowered her voice and said, “Shouldn’t you check with Rachael first? She owns this place, right?”

Right. Rachael did own the island and the hotel. I’d gifted them to her so my father couldn’t take them along with every other property I owned. He’d lied about putting Rocha Enterprises, the company my grandfather left me in his will, into my name when I graduated. Since it was still in his name when I built it to its billion-dollar status, he thought he had the right to take it all away from me. Turtle

Tear was more Rachael's than mine from the beginning. If any of my properties were going to be saved from Enzo's greedy fingers, it was Turtle Tear.

Since the island and hotel were hers, if she wasn't happy with Nadia being here, was it fair of me to expect her to let her stay? Was it fair to Nadia to make her be here where she wasn't wanted? Should I be here causing this for both of them?

Maybe Beck was right. Divide and conquer. I could take Nadia and go away for a while, take a long vacation somewhere. Let Rachael have some time to get used to the idea of me coming with not just MJ, but Nadia as well.

I couldn't change that, so something had to give.

"Dad?" Nadia said when I didn't answer.

"I'll talk to her. I'm sure we'll figure things out. I know it hasn't been easy for either of you."

"I'm trying," she whispered. "She hates me."

"She doesn't. We need to talk about your relationship with your grandfather. Having a better understanding of where you're coming from will go a long way with Rachael. Tomorrow, when everyone else is gone, the three of us will sit down and have a talk about everything."

She stared into the fire and nodded. "Okay."

Step One: Communication. Something I'd never been very good at, but if I was going to be the best husband I could be like I'd promised, getting everything out into the open was key.

A little while later, we helped our guests gather their

suitcases and headed to the landing pad. Beck, Paul, and I loaded the helicopter while the women said good-bye. I knew Rachael would be teary when her mom and Jan left, and it was hard for me to see her upset when I couldn't do anything to fix it but tell her they'd be back soon and she could visit whenever she wanted to make the trip. If I told her that now, though, she'd think I was trying to get rid of her.

Constantly avoiding land mines—this was my life now.

"Take it easy. Come see us soon." Beck grasped my hand and we shook and patted each other on the back.

"We'll be up soon. Tell that son of mine I hope he got a good grade on that exam he bolted out of here to study for."

"Will do." Beck held up a hand to wave at Joan. "Time to go!"

She herded Sylvia and Jan to the helicopter, Rachael following along looking forlorn. They drove her crazy half the time they were here, but when they left, it killed her.

I shook Paul's hand. "I won't think this good-bye is for good this time. Come back whenever you want."

"Thank you for having me. Come back to France and stay with us again."

"We will. Tell your mom and dad hello for me." I stepped back and let Nadia say her good-bye, turning away when the kissing began. What I assumed a father should feel seeing his daughter kiss a man—a sort of anger washed with embarrassment for both of us—wasn't what I was feeling, but there was something nagging about seeing it.

When they were all tucked inside, Rachael, Nadia, and I stood back. Beck lifted the helicopter off the ground and they were gone.

I put one arm around Rachael and the other around Nadia. "Just me and my two girls." Both of them needed cheering up from seeing their loved ones depart. "How about we go back and make s'mores?"

"I've got a headache," Rachael said. "I'm going to go upstairs and lie down."

"I'm on a diet," Nadia said. "I'll sit with you if you want to make some for yourself."

I recognized this test for what it was, and there was no way I was going to fall for either of their traps. Going upstairs was picking Rachael, and staying by the fire was picking Nadia. "You know," I said, "I think I'll find Mr. Simcoe and see if he wants to pick up our game of chess from earlier in the week."

Back at the hotel, I left them both and went in search of solitude. I did need to get away and take a vacation—alone.

Twenty-Four

Rachael

Merrick wasn't going to find Mr. Simcoe; he was escaping the two of us. Who did he think he was fooling?

I rested for about five minutes, but the thoughts running rampant through my mind wouldn't let me nap. My head was aching, so I got up to get the aspirin out of the medicine cabinet in the hall bathroom. Halfway there, I heard Nadia talking to someone behind the closed bathroom door.

Knowing I shouldn't eavesdrop on her conversation didn't stop me from creeping closer and straining to hear what she was saying. Some people needed to be listened to, and if she was on the phone with her mother or Enzo, I wanted to hear every word.

She stopped speaking, and I thought she'd hung up. I was about to tiptoe away when I heard her again. "I'm not going to tell him," she said. "I have something to benefit by this, too, you know."

It took every ounce of willpower I had not to go charging in there and demand to know what she was talking about, but I knew that would only push Merrick and he needed to be eased into the revelation that his daughter was a manipulative mastermind like her grandfather. Instead, I tucked the information away and made my way back to our bedroom. I'd talk to him about it, but I had to do it when the time was right so he didn't think I was attacking him with accusations about Nadia.

As I stared out the bedroom window, my mind raced. She had to have been talking about Merrick. She'd said she didn't want him to know something. Who else would she be talking about? Paul? Enzo?

No. Just as I'd suspected all along, Nadia knew something that Enzo and Gina didn't want Merrick to know.

I tapped my nails on the windowsill. Back in France, on the phone, Nadia had told me she wanted to do what was right. It was clear from what I'd just heard that she was lying. My best move would be to try to gain her confidence and try to pry the truth from her.

That was my best bet to get this situation under control. My mom always told me you win more bees with honey that you do with vinegar. I guess I'd been going about this all wrong with Nadia. I needed to spread the honey on thick. The dress shopping backfired, but now we were stuck together without anyone but Merrick and Mr. Simcoe to play referee between us. It was time for some female bonding. I only wish I'd spent more time at parties and sleepovers when I was young and less time daydreaming about redesigning Barbie's dream home.

The second part of my plan would be even harder. I had to get rid of Merrick for a few hours. Luckily, Beck never turned down my pleas for help.

Merrick came in an hour later when I was under the covers reading. "Couldn't find Mr. Simcoe," he said, pulling his T-shirt over his head.

"It's pretty bad if an old man can escape you on this tiny island." I winked and pulled the blanket back, inviting him to come to bed.

"I swear that man's got a secret hiding spot." He stripped down to his boxer briefs and climbed in beside me. His body was warm and his hair smelled faintly of bonfire. I set my book on the nightstand and turned to him, snuggling against his side. His arms wrapped around me and held me tight. I kissed his bare chest and laid my cheek against it to hear his heart beating.

There was so much to talk about—the potential of him working again someday, Nadia, our wedding, how his visit with Beck went—that it was overwhelming, so I didn't say one word. Neither did Merrick. He ran the tips of his fingers up and down my arm until the stretch of skin underneath went numb, lulling my heavy eyelids closed.

The next afternoon, Merrick found me in the kitchen slicing fruit. "Beck just called," he said. "He wants me to check out this Harley store in Daytona with him. Says it's the biggest store in the U.S."

"Yeah?" I popped a cherry in his mouth. "Sounds like something you'd love. What time are you going?"

"You don't care? I could take Nadia with me."

"No. I don't care." I'd planned it. "Nadia would be bored out of her mind there. We'll watch a movie or something." I rose up on my toes and gave him a kiss. "Don't worry."

He looked hopeful, but leery. "Okay. If you're sure."

"I'm sure."

"We'll leave here in a couple hours then. I'll be back later tonight." He grabbed a handful of cherries and pulled his phone from his pocket. "I'll bring you back some ass-less leather chaps to ride in."

I smiled at his sultry grin. "As long as they have fringe."

"Done."

He strode out of the kitchen dialing Beck. It was time to put the second part of my plan into action.

I found Nadia tanning by the pool and plopped down into the chaise next to her. "This is fabulous, isn't it? Lying in the sun, swimming. I wish there was a pizza place that could deliver out here, though." I laughed and watched the confusion sweep across her face. It wasn't like me to sit down and start chatting with her. She didn't want it and neither did I, but too bad for both of us.

"I was thinking," I continued. "Merrick's going to some big Harley store with Beck later. Maybe we could watch movies? Drink some wine? Have a girls' night and start over. I think we owe it to him to make this work between us."

She gave nothing away, only shrugged. "Sure. Why not. I don't have any other plans."

"Great! We'll make a night of it." I lay back in the sun and closed my eyes, wondering if she'd start a conversation. She made me nervous and that pissed me off. I hated that she held so much sway over Merrick, and I knew she was out to get me. From where I sat, she held every advantage. Sure, Merrick loved me, but he'd tire of having to deal with the bickering between me and Nadia, and he'd already told me not to make him choose.

In all honesty, I'd never been more afraid in my life. What if this caused a rift between him and me that I couldn't bridge because this woman beside me was determined to pry us apart farther and farther until the Grand Canyon stood between Merrick and me?

I couldn't let that happen, but I was grasping at straws trying to prevent it. Her admission that she was holding a secret over us would be my only saving grace.

"You look tense," Nadia said, making my eyes pop open. "I know a good masseuse who has a spa in Miami. He spends half his time there and half in Spain. We should see if we can get in."

I didn't know where this was coming from, but I'd take it. "That sounds perfect. Mr. Simcoe can take us by boat to the mainland and wait there for us to get back. I'll arrange a driver to take us to the spa."

"Perfect! Let me call and get us in. He's booked for months, but always finds a way to squeeze me in."

I watched as she called to make our appointments and hoped I wouldn't end up at the bottom of the river tied to cement blocks.

The hour-and-a-half drive to Miami went fast. Nadia was chatty. She told me about the all-girls schools she'd gone to through the eighth grade. There had been three of them. Two in Spain and one in France. She and Gina moved a lot, all over Europe, so she didn't have many friends. She'd only stayed at the Rocha Estate with Enzo once. It was during the summer and she was kept hidden away in the west wing so MJ wouldn't see her while he was home on break.

No matter what I thought of Nadia, it broke my heart that Enzo—that absolute monster of a man—tore his family apart, robbed them of two decades of knowing and loving each other.

High school had been done online and through homeschooling with a hired teacher who traveled with them. A male hired teacher who, if my deductive reasoning wasn't faulty, she'd screwed six ways to Sunday.

Her life had been luxurious and crazy. Indulgent yet full of sacrifice. She'd had everything a girl could want growing up and nothing she needed. She was the product of raising a child by throwing money at it. No wonder she was so manipulative. She'd had to be to get any attention at all from the sounds of it.

I found myself feeling sorry for her as we pulled up to the spa. Maybe this day would show me a different side to Nadia, and she'd trust me enough to tell me the truth about why she was here and what was going on.

The spa was a modern, pink stucco building with tall, narrow windows and a mirrored door that said *Marcello's* over it on a black script sign. We walked into a dim lobby with a trickling fountain and soft music playing overhead. A petite woman in a black smock rushed toward us. "Welcome to Marcello's! Ms. Rocha and Ms. DeSalvo, correct?"

They must schedule appointments one at a time so they know who's coming in. Or she was telepathic. "That's right," Nadia chirped, putting her high-society face on. "Marcello fit us in today."

"Right this way."

She left us in dressing rooms, or I guess it's more accurate to call them undressing rooms, with fluffy white robes and slippers. I found Nadia already lying naked on her stomach with a sheet covering her bottom half when I came out into the massage room. "Have you had a massage before?" she asked, probably sensing my apprehension at dropping my robe and climbing up on the table.

"No. I've always wanted to get one, though." It wasn't a total lie. Thinking of having the knots and kinks worked out of my muscles was pleasurable enough, but I'd never gotten over how uncomfortable it would be having someone I didn't even know touching my bare skin.

"Well, I'll turn my head while you lie on your table and pull the sheet up. Don't worry, you're going to love it."

I lost track of time, but what seemed like hours later, hot stones where being lined up along my spine. I was loose and jelly-like. My thoughts roamed to Nadia and how we got along when she was telling me how things should be. Like with Merrick and encouraging him to build his business again. Whether her motivation was simply an unconscious desire for having control since she never had any with Enzo and Gina, or if what she was leading me toward was part of a plan, I had no idea. If I wanted to get along with her, I'd let her call the shots. After overhearing her phone conversation, I was going in with my eyes open and would give her the sense that I would do whatever she wanted. Hopefully, that would reveal enough to get me to the truth.

The massage therapists left the room to let our bodies soak in the heat from the stones. With no one else in the room, it was time to dive into Nadia's psyche. "Do you and your mom get along well?" I asked.

"Yes. She has high expectations, but she's pretty much all I've ever had."

"It had to be hard keeping the secret that she was alive all those years. That had to be a lot to take on as a kid."

My face was resting in the hole in the cushion, so I could only see the floor, but I heard her shift on her table. "Well, I didn't know she was supposed to be dead until

I was older. It wasn't that hard considering nobody knew I existed either. We were living our own private lives in Europe, so it wasn't ever a problem."

"True. I guess that would make it a little easier."

"You don't know your family has...issues or whatever when it's the only thing you know. It was always normal to me."

Now we were closing in on a groundbreaking discussion. "What about now? I remember when you and I were on the phone when Merrick and I were at the hotel in Paris. You mentioned wanting to do what was right. What did you mean by that?"

I held my breath waiting for her reply and hoped I hadn't pounced to fast.

"Oh, Rachael, you and I both know I kept the secret that MJ and I were my dad's kids for Enzo. I didn't want to stay with my grandfather and make it seem like I was picking him over my dad."

She was good. She kept up her story. I wanted so badly to push her, but it was too soon. I needed more bonding time. Maybe just questioning for clarification would be enough to open her up more. "I've been wondering...why did you tell Merrick about you and MJ being his kids and Gina being alive? You came to the island a few months ago to protect that secret, right? So why did you end up telling him everything?"

Nadia stiffened, bristled. My direct approach had struck a chord. "I was pissed," she said. "I still am. Enzo promised me something that I found out he couldn't deliver on, so if he wasn't going to keep up his end of the bargain, then I wasn't either."

"Oh." Now it was clear. She did it to strike back at Enzo for screwing her over. This was more in character for the Nadia I knew. But what did she want that she didn't get? Should I come right out and ask?

The door opened and the message therapists came back in, ending my dilemma. I'd keep that information tucked into the back of my mind and try to figure out what it was that Nadia wanted that made her turn on her grandfather. Whatever it was, it would be good for Merrick to know about.

Our session ended on Marcello's balcony, where we ate sparse salads with spiky lettuce dressed in lemon juice. As I was a woman who liked to really eat when I ate, this wasn't going to cut it for me. The view of the ocean with waves crashing in on the beach was amazing, though, and the massage had done wonders relaxing me.

"Thanks for suggesting this," I said, "and getting us in. I really enjoyed it."

"You're welcome. I figured if you were trying to be nice to me, I'd do the same for my dad's sake. I don't want him to think I'm not doing my part to play nice."

The fact that her compliments came wrapped in barbed wire did little to endear her to me. I stabbed a forkful of bitter lettuce and swallowed it down. It was already six in the evening and I was ready to get home. "I'm in the mood to watch a romantic comedy tonight. What do you think?" I frowned down at my wilted lettuce. "I'm taking a pizza back with us, too."

She stretched and yawned. "Sure. I might not make it through a movie, but why not?"

Her yawn was contagious. We both fell asleep in the back of the car on the way to the dock to meet Mr. Simcoe. The boat ride reinvigorated us, though, with the cool night air blowing against our faces. By the time we got back to Turtle Tear, the pizza was cold, but neither of us cared and each scarfed down a piece in the golf cart on the way to the hotel.

Once we'd gone upstairs and changed, I popped the DVD in and we settled onto one of the leather couches in the lounge to eat and watch the movie. It was an odd feeling being with Nadia and not just because I didn't trust her. She wasn't much younger than me, but because I was engaged to her father, it was different than hanging out with a friend. We weren't friends, and with the dynamics of our relationship, we never would be.

After a while, I gathered the courage to confront her with a question I already thought I had the answer to. "Nadia, why don't you want your dad to marry me?"

She gave me the sweetest smile. "Rachael, I guess I'm still like a little girl in that respect. I never stopped wanting my dad and mom to get together."

My pizza turned to cement in my stomach. That was what this was about? Her master plan was to get Gina and Merrick together?

Nadia wasn't a sentimental little sap. If she wanted them together, there was a reason. "Well, it's not going to come as a surprise that we want different outcomes. I'm planning on marrying your father and nothing will change that." Not even her tactics to make me into the evil stepmom.

She only smiled sweetly again, but I saw that sharp edge gleaming in her eyes.

I suffered through the rest of the movie, then stood up to get the hell out of there. "I'm exhausted, going up to bed. See you in the morning."

"Sweet dreams," she said, almost like a taunt. "I'll let my dad know what a great time we had when he gets home."

Was I supposed to be worried that she was waiting up for him? Should I be? I couldn't keep up with my head spinning with questions. I held up my hand and waved good night as I left the lounge.

Upstairs, I sorted through all the puzzle pieces of Nadia. What fit together and what was missing? What I knew: She was sucking up to Merrick, she wanted Merrick to rebuild his company, she had interest in what MJ was doing with the Weston Plantation, she wanted her mom and Merrick together, and she wanted something from Enzo that he didn't give her.

The easy fit was having her mom and dad married when

he rebuilt Rocha Enterprises. She would reap the benefits of inheriting the company someday. If I was in the picture as his wife, I would get it, and if I didn't like her, she wouldn't see a dime.

But there was something else. This nagging feeling that I was missing a major part of the picture wouldn't leave me. How did Enzo fit into this? His hand was always the one moving the pieces around the board. What would he get out of Gina and Merrick being together? Or would he be screwed over somehow? Was Nadia still trying to retaliate against him?

My brain was still churning when Merrick came in with Harley-Davidson bags. "Hey," I said, sitting up, "have a good time?"

"Yeah, we had a great time." He set the bags on the end of the bed and grabbed me, pulling me to him and kissing me like he hadn't seen me in a week. "I missed you."

"I guess you did." My lips tingled and the warm tickle of pleasure was spreading between my legs.

"I'm glad you're still awake." He playfully nipped my bottom lip and tugged.

"I think I'm about to be very happy I'm still awake."

He pulled the covers back and grabbed my sleeping shorts by the waistband. "Yes, you are." The shorts were disposed of and he was rattling around in one of the bags. "Put these on."

He handed me a pile of folded black leather. "What is this?" My eyes widened as I unfolded the item.

"Ass-less leather chaps. I told you I was going to get you a pair."

"Holy hell." They were black and laced up the thighs. "You actually did, too."

He chuckled. "How 'bout that?"

"Yeah, how about that?"

Merrick pulled me to my feet and slapped my ass. "Put them on!"

"Okay." I was all for dressing sexy for my man, but ass-less leather chaps were out of my realm. What the hell? He was all into his biker thing now, so I'd play along.

I took my new chaps into the adjoining bathroom and closed the door. If he wanted biker chick, well, I'd give him my version of biker chick. I lost my panties and figured out which laces and zippers went where. They were tight and felt like I'd shoved my legs into leather gloves, but they were soft and not uncomfortable.

Luckily, I'd hung a lacy red bra on the back of the bathroom door a while ago and forgot about it. I shed my T-shirt and put it on. "Time to look a little trashy," I said, picking up a comb and teasing my hair. I sprayed it, making it puffy, then put on thick black eyeliner, mascara, and red lipstick.

Standing back admiring myself in the mirror, I had to admit I was hot. Merrick was going to go crazy.

I cracked the bathroom door. "Close your eyes."

"They're closed."

"How do I know they're closed?" I laughed. "Okay, keep them that way. I'm coming out."

He stood beside the bed in just his jeans. They were unbuttoned and his feet were bare. His eyes were closed tight and I had an idea. "Don't move," I said.

Digging through the Harley-Davidson bags, I found exactly what I figured I'd find. A black Harley bandanna with an eagle and the logo on it. I stood on the bed, rolled it, and secured it around his head over his eyes.

"What are you doing?" he asked, reaching up to grasp it as I tied it tight.

"Playing. Are you afraid?"

"No, I'm not afraid," he said in a teasing voice. "But I wanted to see you in these." He grabbed my butt and squeezed.

"You will. When it's time." I hopped down to the floor and stood back, taking him in. I still couldn't understand how this man had fallen in love with me. I mean, I was attractive and smart, but he could have models, anyone really. His body was beautiful, cut and strong. He was talented and a brilliant businessman, and his heart... his heart was kind and generous. He loved with everything he had, sometimes to a fault.

"Did you leave?" he asked, reaching out for me.

I took his hand and kissed his fingertips. "No. Just admiring you. Nobody else can ever have you."

He cupped my neck and pulled me in. "Of course nobody else can have me. Hate to break it to you, but you're stuck with mc until the day I die."

I broke off his laugh by sucking on his bottom lip. He

kneaded my bare ass cheeks as I kissed down his chest and left red lipstick prints. I unzipped him and pushed his jeans down. He stepped out of them and kicked them aside. I'd never left a lipstick ring around a man's penis before, and was anxious to do it to Merrick.

I dropped to my knees and he held my head in his hands. I'd never wanted to pleasure a man with my mouth as much as I did him. In the past, with other guys I'd gone out with, I'd done it when I felt like I had to, like repaying them for going down on me. With Merrick, I loved it. I loved how much *he* loved it. Turning him on turned me on.

I stroked him lightly, kissing the inside of his thigh. His knees bent a little in anticipation. I turned him so he backed up against the bed. "Sit and lie back," I said, pushing him down.

On my knees, I positioned myself between his long legs. His balls were full and heavy, his cock erect and standing away from his stomach. I ran my nose up and down its length, letting my hands slide up over his abdomen. He felt so good under my hands, so solid and... *mine*. Having him like this grounded me. When there was nothing but questions all day long, there was this at night. Us. Together. No questions, just instinct.

He groaned. I could tell he was going crazy waiting for me to take him into my mouth. I touched the base of him with the tip of my tongue and slowly licked upward to his tip. He breathed deep and bunched the quilt in his hands. "Is it different when you can't see anything?" I asked.

"It's amazing, but it's always amazing."

I ran my tongue under the ridge around his head, then put it in my mouth and wrapped my lips around him. I didn't move, just massaged him with my tongue. His hands came up; his fingers threaded in my hair. I knew he wanted to push me down farther, but he didn't. I wanted to make him wild, and it was working.

"You're being a tease," he said. "First you don't let me see you wearing my present; now this." He sat up and pushed the bandanna up onto his forehead. "I'm not going to lie here and take it, Ms. DeSalvo. This ass is mine." He grabbed my butt and pulled me onto his lap, straddling him. "And I want to see it."

He rubbed a thumb over my bottom lip. "Look at you. Mmm." His fingers crawled deeper and lower between my legs from behind. Finding me wet and swollen, Merrick moaned and lay back on the bed. He cocked his finger, beckoning me to crawl higher. "On my face. You're dressed for a ride and I'm going to take you on one."

He grabbed my hips and positioned me so I was spread over his mouth. I braced my palms against the wall in front of me and felt him slide his finger inside. His tongue explored my slick folds, flicking and laving, making me dig my nails into the drywall. It was payback time and he was avoiding the one sweet spot I needed him to suck. "Who's the tease now?"

As soon as the words were out, he latched on with his lips and sucked me relentlessly, plunging a second finger in with the first and working them back and forth, bending his fingers. The tender, prickling heat grew in intensity, the flames licking higher, ready to burn me to ash. I ground against his mouth and urged it to come faster. My muscles clenched. I gritted my teeth and silently chanted, yes, yes, yes! It hit with a ferociousness that pulled me down against the wall, whimpering in surrender.

Merrick released me and cradled me in his arms. "Who likes ass-less chaps now?" he chuckled and kissed me, leaving salty traces of me on my lips.

"I love ass-less chaps," I said, breathless.

"The ride's not over yet, you know."

I grabbed his rock-hard cock and nodded. "I know. This is the *big* race, too." I climbed on top of him and pushed his shoulders back onto the bed. "You better put the key in the ignition."

He grabbed himself and slid his head up and down through my folds, between my ass cheeks and back again before nestling himself at my opening. "I'm ready to fire the starting pistol."

I giggled. "Okay, enough with that." Lowering down onto him, the overwhelming sensation of oneness and belonging took me over. So full. So complete. So perfect. "I love this so much," I said, beginning to ride him. I took him deep and rose until he was almost out of me before pushing back down again. I went slow, grinding forward and back, then faster, up and down, circling my hips, pressing my hands against his chest. I wanted to come again, but this time was all about him.

I watched his face, listened for his breath hitching and quickening, felt for the grasp of his hands, digging into my hips, guiding me, urging me on, faster and harder. "I can't—God—Rachael!" He grunted and bit his lip, his eyes squeezed tight and his dick thickened. His excitement and the pressure building more friction inside me brought me to the edge again. I wanted it so badly and I wanted to come with him. I reached between my legs and rubbed my fingers in fast circles, both of us bucking and thrusting. I closed my eyes against the blur of orgasm and felt him throbbing and pulsing into me as my own contractions squeezed around him.

Spent and panting heavily, I lay on Merrick's chest as he scratched my back in lazy circles. "I love you," I said. "Best gift ever."

Twenty-Five

Merrick

Nadia was awake and making breakfast in the kitchen when I came down early, leaving Rachael asleep. "Morning!" she said, pouring me a cup of coffee. "I've got pancakes and sausage almost ready."

"It smells incredible. My stomach's growling. Can I help with anything?"

She waved her spatula at me. "Nope. Just sit and relax."

I grabbed my phone and started scanning through e-mails. "How was your day yesterday? What did you do?" Probably avoided Rachael, and I was sure the same would be true about my lovely fiancée.

"Rachael and I went to Miami to this amazing spa—I know the owner so he got us in last minute. We got massages and had a girls' day."

I couldn't be hearing this right. "A girls' day? You and Rachael?"

She nodded enthusiastically and turned back to the stove to flip pancakes. "Then we came back, ate pizza, and watched a movie."

"You and Rachael? Seriously? Wow. I can't tell you how

happy that makes me." I could actually feel the weight lifting off my shoulders. If they got along, my life would be perfect.

"I know. We both want you to be happy, so we're trying." She plated my breakfast, picked up a jug of maple syrup off the counter, and brought it to me at the table.

"Thanks. It looks great." I picked up my fork and dug in.

Nadia slid onto the chair across from me and watched me chew. She stared at me kind of starry-eyed, like a young girl who admired her father might. It was crazy and fantastic and a little strange all at the same time. "Aren't you eating?" I asked her.

"I had some fruit."

"Did Paul get back okay?"

She twirled her hair around her finger. "Yeah. I talked to him last night and told him you were at the Harley store." She laughed. "He said he wants a picture of you with a bandanna around your head."

My mind flashed back to last night when Rachael blindfolded me with it. I made a point to look down into my plate and chuckle like I hadn't just had erotic memories that were giving me half wood. "Planning to see him again soon?"

She sighed. "I don't know. I'm sure I'll see him again, but an intercontinental romance is pretty impossible."

I thought about how Rachael and I began. "Nothing's impossible if you want it enough."

With a far-off look in her eyes, she gazed out the window.

"Some things seem pretty impossible when they're out of your control."

Somehow I didn't think we were talking about Paul anymore. I was no stranger to feeling out of control when I was her age. "You take what you want, no matter the cost." That sounded like good dad advice. Not that I'd ever received good dad advice myself, but I could wing it.

"Lie, cheat, and steal, just don't get caught?" She grinned.

I shook my head, standing with my empty plate. "Yeah, something like that." She was a character. I'm glad we could joke around like this after our rocky start a few months ago.

"In that case," she said, following me over to the sink, "I have something to tell you. I think you'll be okay with it. It's not a big deal really..."

Why did this sound like I was being led to the dungeons? "Okay."

"My mom's going to come visit and apologize for going along with Enzo all those years."

"Gina?" All of the air rushed out of me. "When?"

"This afternoon." She bit the inside of her cheek. "Unless you want me to tell her not to come."

Fuck. *Fuckfuckfuck.* Turning down an apology would make me the asshole in this situation. Rachael was going to go through the roof. "No, it's fine." I managed a smile for Nadia's sake. "It'll be good to clear the air. We have kids together after all."

The truth of my statement sent me reeling. We had kids together. We'd forever be tied by them. She was in my life whether I wanted her to be or not. Our kids would have kids—our grandkids. Birthdays and baptisms and holidays with Gina Montgomery flashed through my mind. I'd never be free of her. And to think, only a few months ago I thought she was dead. Talk about your life-altering revelations.

We heard the helicopter approaching at three o'clock that afternoon. Rachael stood on one side of me, pissed enough to kick kittens, and Nadia bounced on her toes on the other side, shading her eyes to get a glimpse of the copter.

"I cannot *fucking* believe this," Rachael muttered, too low for Nadia to hear.

I took her hand and whispered, "I'll make it up to you." I wished I knew how.

When I went upstairs after breakfast and told her Gina was coming today, I swear fire was going to shoot from her eyes. She screamed into her pillow and threw it at me. Then she stopped speaking altogether. I guessed she was too pissed to form words.

The private-piloted helicopter Gina had hired touched down. We waited for the propellers to slow before going near. Rachael kept a death grip on my hand. I was fine with that. I'd rather have her hold on than let go.

The pilot got out first and rounded to the passenger side. When he came back around, he escorted a petite blonde in a pink sundress with black sunglasses on. I never would recognize her if I ran into her. Not in a million years. The way she sashayed across the grass toward us, she wasn't the sunny-dispositioned girl who used to babysit me and my sister. She was a woman on a mission. I didn't like what my senses were telling about that mission.

When she reached me, she ripped her sunglasses from her eyes and shook out her hair. "Little Merrick, my, have you grown into a fine-looking man." Her smile spoke of shared secrets. What we shared wasn't a secret any longer. "I saw your sister not too long ago. She's doing well. And that niece and nephew of yours! Adorable!" She turned her eyes to Nadia and reached out to hug her. "Hello, darling girl. I've missed you."

With no way to ignore Rachael any longer, Gina turned her attention to her. "You must be the fiancée I've heard so much about." She held out a hand to shake Rachael's. Rachael took it, but looked like she'd swallowed something that made her sick to her stomach. "Gina Montgomery. Nice to meet you."

I should've introduced them, but I hadn't said a word. I was such an idiot. "This is Rachael DeSalvo," I said—finally.

"Nadia told me she ruined your dress," Gina said to Rachael with a frown and a *tsk* sound. "Such a shame."

Rachael inhaled sharply, but maintained her composure. "That's okay. It was just a dress." She looked up at me and ran her hand up my arm. "It wasn't what will make the day special anyway."

That's my girl. I hooked my arm around her waist and pulled her against my side. "No, it's not what you wear that matters, but I know you'll find something lovely to replace it."

"Is Nadia in the wedding?" Gina asked, looking from one to the other of the three of us in turn.

"We hadn't—" I said. "I was thinking—" Rachael said at the same time.

"No," Nadia answered. "It's Rachael's day and her attendants should be people she's close to."

Gina eyed me sternly for a second. She didn't need to. I felt like shit already. My daughter wouldn't be in my wedding when her twin brother was my best man. "I want you to be in it," I told her, ignoring the daggers being stared into my back by Rachael. "We'll find a role for you to fill."

"She's too old for flower girl!" Gina laughed and tapped her lips with the end of the arm of her sunglasses. "Well, I could use a drink. How about showing me around?" Her question was clearly directed at me. "I figure we have some things to discuss," she said, dismissing Rachael with a tight-lipped smile and curt nod.

Rachael wasn't a docile woman to be played like this, but the situation was such an odd one, she looked up at me, eyes blank, giving nothing away, and said, "Of course. Let's get your things situated and Merrick can make you a drink and show you around my island."

My island. I see. It was her way of pissing in the corners to mark her territory, so to speak. I hope she didn't feel like she needed to mark me, too. I belonged to her one hundred percent and always would.

Gina let out a big, bold laugh. "Oh! Have you two signed the prenup then? What's yours is yours and will remain so," she said, vibrant eyes twinkling at Rachael. "I don't blame you. A woman has to protect herself financially."

Said the woman who made a career out of pretending to be dead for twenty years. Rachael didn't say a word, just kept right on smiling with that nothingness in her eyes, like she'd left the building and was staying gone until Gina flew out of here.

I met the pilot halfway to the helicopter and took Gina's suitcase, wondering how long she was staying because it weighed a ton. It would be rude to ask. I mean, she raised my daughter. I could at least host her for a day or two. Although I hoped she'd be leaving in the morning if not sooner.

I drove the four of us to the hotel and showed Gina to the room beside Nadia's. She looked around like she couldn't believe she was staying here in this hotel that wasn't the Four Seasons or a five-star property. "It's... quaint, isn't it?" She fingered a lace doily on the nightstand.

"I suppose it is." I set her suitcase beside the bed. "We wanted it to look as original as possible. This place holds a lot of special meaning for Rachael and me."

"That's sweet." She kicked off her shoes. "I'll just change and meet you in the kitchen then for that drink?"

"Sounds good." I couldn't get out of there fast enough. This was going to be a very long evening.

Downstairs in the kitchen, Rachael had already made drinks for all of us. "Mojitos," she said, garnishing them with lime wedges.

I walked around behind her at the island and took her in my arms. "Thank you. I never imagined I'd have to ask so much from you. I know this isn't easy." I kissed the back of her neck, thankful that she put her hair up and gave me free access. "Just keep telling yourself that you're the love of my life and soon we'll be married and nothing else matters."

"Is that how you feel?" She sliced another lime in half. "Because they will forever be a part of our lives. It's not going to change."

Panic started to creep in. I turned her around to face me, took the knife from her hand, and set it on the counter. "Are you trying to tell me something? Is this too much for you?"

She wouldn't look at me. "No. I'm not telling you anything except how it is. You do realize that when she leaves and when Nadia leaves—if she ever does—it's not over. There's no over to this." Then she lifted her eyes, like black, soulless rocks, to mine. "It will always matter."

This was killing her.

"Ah, drinks!" Gina said, strolling into the kitchen.

I gave Rachael a quick kiss. "We'll talk later."

"Can we take our drinks with us? Are we walking or taking a golf cart around the island?" Gina picked up a glass and took a sip. "Delicious. Did you make these, Merrick?"

"Ah, no. Rachael made them." I didn't want to leave her like this. She was scaring the hell out of me. The only safety net I had was being on an island. It wasn't like she could get in her car and drive away while I was giving the grand tour of the place.

"Well, they're great. Were you a barmaid?" Gina asked her.

Jesus. "No. Rachael is an architect and designer. She was the project manager on the restoration of this hotel and island."

"Oh, that's right." Gina ran her tongue across her front teeth. "I did hear something about that."

Rachael picked up her drink. "Well, I'll let you two get to it."

She stepped away and I squeezed her shoulder. "We'll be back soon. I'll make your favorite for dinner."

"Okay." She flashed me a quick, tight smile before striding out of the room.

Gina watched her go, shaking her head. "She's not happy with me being here. I'm sorry. I should've spoken to you first, but Nadia assured me Rachael was okay with everything."

I tossed back half of my mojito. "Well, yesterday they went to the spa together, so things are looking up. You're arrival was a surprise to us both."

She let out an exasperated breath. "I'm sorry. That daughter of ours. She has it in her head that we'll somehow end up together and she'll have the big, happy family she's always wanted."

"Oh?" My stomach lurched like I'd been kicked. I took another healthy gulp of my drink. At the rate this conversation was going, I'd need a few more to take with us on the tour.

"She's a dreamer, our Nadia." She ran her fingertips, caressing, over the countertop. "Always has been." She tossed her head back, her eyes lost in the past. "I have so much to tell you about her childhood. So much you missed. And then there's MJ. We both missed out on his childhood. Not that either of us were given a choice. He was taken from me and sent to live with another woman—a nanny—who raised him. Your father wouldn't let me see him." Her bottom lip quivered and she raised her glass to her mouth. "I'll never forgive Enzo for that."

This was too much, too fast. I was a drowning man. Rachael was my life preserver, but she'd gone back to shore without me. Nothing to do but doggie paddle and try to keep my head above water until this was over.

It would never be over.

God. Rachael was right. This was only the beginning of a lifetime of Gina and Nadia. Hell, they'd fly Enzo in next and really drop a bomb in my lap.

"Well," she said, and patted the countertop. "Let's get going. I want to see everything there is to see here."

"Sure. Is Nadia coming along?" I needed a buffer. We walked down the hall into the lounge.

"No. She's calling her friend Paul. They have a budding romance, I hear. Do you like him?"

Paul? Hadn't they spoken about him this morning? Nadia hadn't seemed anxious to talk with him again. "Yeah, Paul's a good guy."

"Good family?"

"They're very nice." I was sure she was referring to their bank account, but I wasn't going to play into that line of questioning. "We'll take the golf cart." The faster we got this over with, the better.

We crossed the patio and climbed in the cart I'd left parked by the gate. I took off toward the orchard in front of the hotel. According to Nadia, the point of her coming was to apologize for making me think she'd died in childbirth all those years ago. When was that going to come up? "So," I said, figuring I'd air out the dirty laundry, "you're alive."

"I'm alive."

I waited for more, but she said nothing else. "You've been in Europe, I hear."

"Yes." She pointed out of the side of the cart. "Are those key limes trees?"

"They are." We rode along in silence for a few minutes.

"Was Nadia incorrect then," she said, "about the reason I was to come here?"

All I could do was blink. "I'm sorry. I didn't know there was a reason she'd given you. I was told you wanted to come to apologize to me."

She turned her body toward me, gripping the seat with one hand and bracing the other on the windshield. "Apologize! To you? You were the one who was supposed to be doing the apologizing!"

"For what?" I slammed my foot down on the break. "I'm not the one who played dead for twenty years and didn't tell me we had two kids. I missed everything with them, Gina. I carried around the guilt of your death all of those years." I tore my hands through my hair. "Jesus. Apologize to you."

"No! You're not the one who had to go into hiding and care for a newborn and lose her family and her entire life. You're just the one who knocked me up!"

I pounded my hand on the steering wheel. "I didn't make that decision! I didn't pay your family off! I had no idea—Enzo said he handled it when he found out you were pregnant. Nobody asked me what I wanted to do."

She sat back, stared straight ahead, and crossed her arms. "So you're not sorry then."

"As sorry as you seem to be." I slammed the cart back in gear and pressed down on the accelerator.

I couldn't remember the last time I'd been this irritated. It was a waste being mad. What was the point? I didn't care enough about what she thought to be pissed.

Nadia was a different story. Trying to get her mother and me together again was bad enough. Doing it by manipulating us was out of line.

I could only imagine what Rachael would think. Should I even tell her? I didn't want to keep things from her, but she was already in a bad place with this situation. Why add fuel to the fire? Of course, if she found out and I hadn't told her, she'd never forgive me.

All I wanted was to have a peaceful life on Turtle Tear with the woman who would soon be my wife. Was that too much to ask?

Twenty-Six

Rachael

Merrick came storming in through the patio door and strode through the lounge, not stopping for a second. I got up and followed him down the hall into the entryway and up the stairs to our bedroom.

"Didn't go well?" I shut the door behind me. He collapsed back on the bed and rested his forearm over his eyes.

"Are you talking to me now?"

"Did you expect me to be happy about Gina coming here?" I stood beside the bed and looked down at him. He didn't move his arm.

"Did you expect *me* to be happy about it?"

"You could at least tell me why she's here!" I shoved his arm off his face, making him look at me.

He scowled. "I sure as hell didn't invite her if that's what you think."

"I didn't say I thought anything. Why are you pissed at *me* for this? *I'm* the one who gets to be pissed!"

He shot up off the bed. "You get to be pissed, huh? Because all of this is happening to you? Nothing is affecting me? I'm just here to play peacemaker with you and Nadia.

Now Gina shows up and you completely turn on me. That's really fucking fair, Rachael."

"Don't you dare act like I'm not supportive!" He turned away. I grabbed his arm and tried to yank him back around, but he resisted. "Look at me! You don't think I know what this is doing to you?"

He glanced back over his shoulder. "You know. You're more concerned about what it's doing to you."

I was stunned. "You know what? Fuck you. I've done nothing but hold my tongue around you. Nadia is a conniving little bitch who's trying to get you and Gina together."

"I know," he said, like it was no big deal.

"You know? And you still don't think I have a right to be pissed? She's encouraging you to rebuild your company and get with her mother so she can inherit it when you die. What do you think of your precious daughter now?" I flung the words at him like spikes.

His eyes flamed. "I think she's troubled, and being brought up how she was, I'm not surprised. She wants a family who she can depend on. I know how that feels."

I stared right back with equal heat in my eyes. "Where do I fit into this perfect family, Merrick? Or don't I?"

Tiredness washed over his face. "That's up to you. I can't make you want to be a part of my life with Nadia and Gina in it. You said it yourself—this is how it's going to be. It will never be over."

My heart clenched. "You think I don't want to be part of your life?"

"I don't know what to think anymore. I know I can't force you and Nadia together and keeping the two of you apart is exhausting. Just when I think things are looking up and you two have a spa day, she has Gina show up here with the intention of getting us together." He shook his head and sat on the edge of the bed looking down at the floor. "I can't win. There's no coming out of this without hurting one of you."

Hope drained out of me, leaving a gaping hole of emptiness. "So it's going to be me that gets hurt, isn't it?"

"I told you. Don't make me choose."

"What are you saying?" I whispered.

"I'm saying you need to decide what you want, Rachael." He looked up at me with dark, miserable eyes. "Until you do, we need to postpone the wedding plans."

The ring around my finger felt like a brand, digging into my finger, burning and leaving a band of scar tissue. I moved to take it off, but he grasped my hands. "I'm not saying take the ring off. I'm saying we need to put things on hold until you've had time to think about if this is what you want."

I wanted to scream, *Of course this is what I want!* But what I wanted was for him to realize that Nadia was trying to manipulate him somehow. I wish I knew what she was up to, but even if I did, I didn't think it would matter. He knew she was trying to get him and Gina together and he identified with how she felt. Would he go along with it to make her happy? Was that where this was leading? "Do you want to be with Gina?"

He let out a sad chuckle, like he'd given up and was pacifying me by answering my idiotic question. "No, I don't want to be with Gina."

"Will you do it anyway? To make Nadia happy?" I shouldn't have asked it. I didn't want to know the answer.

He licked his lips and looked away. "Only if you leave me. You're the only woman I'll ever love. If I don't have you, I might as well. It won't matter. It'll make Nadia happy and she'll be the only woman left I care about."

So if I was out of the picture, Nadia would get the family she wanted and Merrick would get to make her happy. "And you'll get to make it up to Gina for having to pretend she was dead all those years while she raised your daughter, right? I'm sure that factors into your martyrdom."

"Martyrdom? Jesus Christ, Rachael, you don't get it at all, do you?" He blinked his eyes, incredulous. "That one event in my past—one sexual encounter with Gina—had an enormous domino effect on everyone. Me, her, MJ, and Nadia—"

"Enzo. Don't forget him. He was behind everything, not you. You didn't make her leave and pretend to be dead. You didn't even know she was pregnant. He told you he took care of the situation."

"He did. In a very fucked-up way."

"Yeah." I felt like an old shirt left out on the line to blow in the wind. Where the hell did this leave me?

Merrick scrubbed his face with his hands. "Tomorrow, I'm going to take Gina and Nadia to the Weston Plantation.

MJ's never met his mom. I'm sure Mr. Simcoe will want to go. You're welcome to come, too, if you want."

What was I, an afterthought? "You're doing it again," I said. "Pushing me away when you should be keeping me close."

"I'm not pushing at all. You have a lot to think about. I love you with my entire heart. You're my life. You know that. But the future looks different for me now, and I don't want to assume you wish to be a part of it."

Something happened on the tour of the island with Gina to set him off like this, to unravel everything he'd wound so tight inside. Now the cord was wrapping around my neck and making it hard to breathe.

My future had been so clear. Merrick and I together and happy here at Turtle Tear, our home that we'd share with the occasional group who came for a special event, like the Nelsons and their family renewing their vows on their fiftieth anniversary. I thought that would be us someday, our grandson walking me down the aisle, Beck old and gray, but still with his long hair pulled back, playing his cello. Merrick, dashing in his tux with his salt-and-pepper hair, tall and tan, handsome as ever, watching me walk down the aisle toward him, ready to vow to love him another fifty years—an eternity if I had it to live.

And now...nothing. The wedding I'd been planning was on hold, possibly indefinitely. The world was upside down, and I had to find the strength to right it.

❀

I walked. It always helped Merrick when he had a lot on his mind. Unfortunately, I only wanted to curl up in a ball under one of the key lime trees and sob. That was where I was when Mr. Simcoe found me.

He sat, slowly easing himself down the tree trunk. "I'm not blind to what's going on here, so I know what the tears are about."

I wiped my eyes and tried to smile, but there was no smile inside me. "I don't know what to do. Everything's falling apart."

He put an arm around me and squeezed my shoulder. "No. It just seems that way. Trouble comes and trouble goes. My wife and I weren't strong enough to get through ours, but I can see the strength in you and Merrick's relationship. This is a bump—a mountain—but you two will get over it together."

"I don't know if that's true anymore. All we've done is fight for weeks. Nadia has torn us apart."

"No. She hasn't. She doesn't have the power to do that. Your relationship comes apart when the two of you let go and don't care anymore. You care. He cares. You love each other. She can't change that."

"I don't know. He feels so guilty for not being around when she was growing up. She wants him to get together with Gina. She wants her family. I can't blame her for that. Who doesn't want their mom and dad together?"

"You know," he said, leaning back against the tree and looking up through the branches, "Maddie always wanted me and her mother to get back together, but the truth is, we would've been miserable. We weren't meant to be together. We had a beautiful daughter out of our short-lived marriage, but we were too different. Wanted different things. Maddie wouldn't have been happy with us together, and Nadia will have to realize Merrick and Gina don't make the family she's always envisioned."

That was it.

Mr. Simcoe was a genius.

All I had to do was get Merrick and Gina together in the same room with Nadia and she'd see how ill fit they were.

At least I hoped it would work that way.

I hugged Mr. Simcoe. "Thank you. I feel a lot better."

"I've had a lot of practice talking to young women, you know. Maddie might not always confide in me, but I know what's going on in her head. You don't raise a daughter on your own without learning a few things." He kissed my forehead. I stood and helped him up.

"As a father," I said, "Merrick's never going to see the fault in Nadia, is he?"

He placed his hands on my shoulders. "He sees it. It's hard to admit your princess is acting like a toad, though. Merrick's a smart man. Trust him. He's more perceptive than he lets on. This will all work out, so don't hide and cry under any more trees."

The next afternoon, Merrick flew us to the Weston Plantation. We landed on the back lawn, where a flagstone walkway had been laid and led to a three-tiered fountain gurgling water. Mums were blooming in explosions of yellow, white, and burgundy in planters lining the walkway up to the big white plantation house.

It would be a beautiful spot for a fall reception. I twisted my ring on my finger and clenched my teeth. I would not tear up.

Beck came out of the large outbuilding that was being turned into a guest house and met us on the walk up to the main house. He glanced from Merrick to me, his brows lowered in concern, but then he held out a hand to Gina. "Beck Tanner."

"This is Gina Montgomery," Merrick said. "MJ and Nadia's mother."

"Nice to meet you, Gina," Beck said.

"Nice to meet you, Beck," she said, her white teeth gleaming in the sun under her dark sunglasses. "Do you work for my son?"

"He's an independent contractor," Merrick answered. "He used to work for me. Now he's my best friend and works with MJ when he needs him."

"Oh! Then you're like family, aren't you?" She hooked her arm through Beck's as we walked.

I'd never seen Beck so uncomfortable. He kept darting apologetic glances my way, like he was consorting with the enemy. I knew Merrick had to have given him the rundown from the day before.

"I know Maddie's cooking up a storm," Mr. Simcoe said,

steering the conversation in a different direction. "She told me this morning she was making ham and corn bread."

"Joan made dessert," Beck said, grinning. "Do me a favor. Pretend it's good and choke it down."

"Is Joan your girlfriend?" Gina asked.

"I, um—yeah."

I wondered if Beck would ever give in to the fact that he actually had genuine feelings for Joan. It was clear to everyone else that he wasn't going to break up with her.

"I can't wait to meet her then," Gina said. "I'm sure we'll get along wonderfully."

I almost laughed out loud. Gina meeting Joan was going to be one of the highlights of my life, I had a feeling.

"Well, everyone's in the kitchen," Beck said as we stepped up the front porch stairs. He opened the front door and ushered us inside the large foyer. "They're here!" he called out.

Maddie came rushing around the corner wiping her hands on a kitchen towel. "Hi!" She gave her dad an enormous hug, then gathered me into her arms. "He loves *you*," she whispered before moving on to give Merrick a hug. I needed Maddie's reassurance. It bolstered me a bit.

Maddie told Nadia hello, but before she could be introduced to Gina, MJ walked through the double French doors from the living room. He stopped when he spotted Gina. Everyone was silent and still while Gina stepped forward and the two stared at each other for a moment.

"Merrick Junior," she said, "you look so much like your

father." She covered her mouth, letting out a delighted laugh. "I shouldn't be surprised." She reached back for Nadia's hand. "Your sister looks just like a Rocha, too. Neither one of you look anything like me."

Keeping Nadia's hand, she led her daughter forward. As Gina neared MJ, he took a couple steps forward, his hands tucked in his pockets. Nadia reached out and gave MJ a one-armed hug. He pulled a hand free and patted her back. "Good to see you," he muttered.

"I never thought I'd get to meet you," Gina said. She reached out to touch his cheek, but he flinched and she put her hand down.

Merrick stepped forward, getting MJ's attention, and nodded for him to greet his mother without the hesitation.

MJ didn't budge.

"Son," Merrick said, "could I speak to you for a minute in the living room?" He strode over to where MJ, Nadia, and Gina—his family—stood and waited for MJ to follow him into the living room.

I'd never felt so out of place in my life. Maddie took my hand and squeezed. "Come on in the kitchen. I've got some drinks and appetizers set out."

Gina and Nadia stood, whispering, outside the French doors. "Are you two coming?" Maddie asked.

"I think we'll stay here and wait for the men to come back out," Gina said.

The men. Like they were hers. One was *mine* and the other had wanted nothing to do with her so far. I didn't know if I should stay and wait, too, or if I was a fifth wheel on their family reunion. Either way, my sense of fight or flight was leading me away to the kitchen. I needed to pick my battles and this wasn't one I wanted a part in.

Joan stood at the stove stirring gravy. "Isn't this a little domestic for you?" I asked, standing beside her.

She had her hair pulled back in a ponytail and wore jeans and a simple blouse. "Don't even get me started. Somehow I can't tell Mads no."

It seemed that *Mads* was a good influence on Joan.

Maddie laughed. "Don't let her fool you. She loves this stuff. She even made a cake."

"I heard you made dessert," I said, winking at Beck. "Somebody couldn't wait to tell us."

"It was a warning," he said, popping a cracker in his mouth.

Joan gave him a playful dirty look. "Where's Merrick and his brood?" she asked, rolling her eyes in sympathy.

"Well..." I began, but Maddie was eager to answer.

"MJ wants nothing to do with Gina," she said. "He and Merrick got in an argument about it on the phone yesterday evening. Merrick thinks he should at least meet her and insisted on bringing her today."

"Wow," I said. "I didn't know."

Maddie lifted a big pile of china plates from one of the cupboards. "MJ said he'd rather think of the woman he thought was dead as his mother than the one who was alive and never tried to contact him."

"Can't blame him," Beck said.

Mr. Simcoe poured himself a cup of coffee and sat at the big farmhouse-style table. "Trouble comes and trouble goes," he said, blowing the steam before taking a sip.

"You keep saying that," Maddie said, "but it hasn't left yet, just brought in backup." She tugged a drawer open and started taking out forks. "I swear if that chick thinks she's turning this place into a golf course, she's got another thing coming."

"MJ won't let that happen," Joan said, turning off the burner and moving the pan of gravy to a potholder on the counter. "Merrick can tell him how great it would be until he's blue in the face. You know he doesn't want that." She picked up a dish towel and wiped her hands. "Hell, Rachael had a conniption when I wanted to have a tag sale to get rid of all the old crap in the outbuildings." She grinned at me with her tongue between her teeth and flicked my hip with the end of the towel.

"Hey!" I laughed and grabbed it from her. "The history of this place can't be destroyed. It's sacred." Ingrid had passed away here. This had been her husband's family home. Their children ran around in these rooms and out on the lawns when they visited their grandparents. Over my dead body was anyone going to hack away at the ground with a golf club.

"Merrick starts talking golf course for real," Joan continued, "and his woman's going to murder him in his sleep."

Beck tossed an olive up and caught it in his mouth. "Merrick needs to get his head out of his ass and—"

"And what?" Merrick said, striding into the kitchen.

"And get in here and eat," Beck said, recovering as best as he could. "I'm starving."

Nadia and Gina followed him in. Gina was patting underneath her eyes with a tissue.

"Where's MJ?" Maddie asked.

"He's uh..." Merrick's lips tightened and he shook his head.

"I'll be right back." Maddie dashed out of the room.

Merrick and I stared at each other. This was going poorly. He'd misjudged MJ. Another one he couldn't make happy. He let a fist fall to the counter in defeat.

"Well, sit down," Joan said, shooing everyone to the table. "We have food getting cold. Beck, get that heavy-ass ham out of the oven, would you please?"

"Yes, ma'am," he said, popping another olive into his mouth.

Merrick grabbed the stack of plates while I gathered knives and spoons from the drawer to set the table with the forks Maddie had put out. Mr. Simcoe sat at one end and we left a place for MJ on the other. Merrick sat to one side of MJ's spot and Maddie would be across from him. I went to sit beside Merrick, but Nadia slid in that chair.

Joan looked at me and opened her eyes wide as if to tell me to do something. I didn't know what to do other than dump Nadia out of the chair. Joan set some napkins on the table. "Oh, Nadia, honey," she said, "you're sitting in Rachael's spot. You're over here." She patted the seat beside Mr. Simcoe.

"I'm sorry," Nadia said, sounding stunned. "I didn't realize there was assigned seating." She started to move, but Merrick grabbed her wrist.

"There isn't," he said. "You're fine. I'm sure Rachael won't mind if you sit beside me."

And there it was. He'd chosen her over me. I had a vision of every single gathering we'd have being like this one. Me shunned to the end of the table, the other side of the room, somewhere out of eyesight and arm's reach of Merrick, while his real family was at his side.

I looked at Mr. Simcoe. Did he think we could make it over this mountain now? He cleared his throat. "Merrick, if I may, I'd love to sit next to your beautiful daughter. I haven't had the chance to spend much time talking to her."

He was being kind, but it made me feel pathetic that he had to look out for me. Merrick should want to sit next to me. My eyes started to water and I blinked furiously. Mr. Simcoe took my hand. "There's this tree outside, near the back of the property. You'll love it. I'll show it to you *after* dinner."

Yes, I could hold the tears at bay until after dinner.

Joan shot me a fierce look, urging me to stand my ground.

"Do you mind sitting by Mr. Simcoe?" Merrick asked Nadia.

She shook her head. "Of course not."

Once we were all finally seated, Maddie and MJ came into the room hand in hand. They took their seats and we picked up our forks, but before we started eating, MJ stood up again.

"I'd like to say something," he said. "I don't know how to feel about this yet." He nodded to his mother. "But you're all welcome here and I'm happy to be sharing my table with all of you. This wasn't a picture that ever entered my mind—my family around the dinner table—but here we are." He picked up his glass, and the rest of us did the same. "To family and friends," he said.

And we drank.

Which was I—family or friend? Or would I end up being neither?

Twenty-Seven

Merrick

Dinner was awkward as hell. I didn't know what Rachael was thinking. When I said we should postpone the wedding, I thought she was going to take her ring off and throw it at me. Thank God I grabbed her hand before she had the chance. I wanted her to tell me I was being crazy, that of course we would get married. To tell me I was being stupid. But I guess the whole reason for proposing that we put it off was because I knew she wasn't ready.

Hell, I'd known that before I proposed.

I should've waited until the dust settled to see if she was still standing beside me, or if I'd lost her in the fallout of this ugly explosion that took over my world.

Now MJ was equally cold toward me. Losing one of them would destroy me. I didn't know what would happen if I lost them both.

Jesus, I just wanted everyone at this table to get along. Why was that too much to ask? My kids, the mother of my kids, my best friend, my fiancée, my someday daughter-in-law and her father, my assistant, hell, my life mentor. And

Joan. All of them were important to me. Why were they looking at me like I was the biggest asshole they'd ever seen? Well, except Nadia and Gina, who both seemed to be convinced that I was the force that made the earth turn. But I knew that was based on the hopes of gaining financially on Gina's part, and who knew what Nadia's true motivation was. I might never know. I didn't really care. She was my daughter and that was all that mattered.

"Aren't you hungry?" Rachael asked.

My plate was practically full. "Not really." She pushed food around her own plate. "Aren't you?"

She shook her head. "No appetite."

I rested my hand on her thigh under the table. Did she think she was losing me? Shit. She had to think that. But was I losing her?

Our relationship was never this hard, and when it was just the two of us, it was easy. Even living on an island didn't isolate us from the real world. If I could put up fences and a dome, live sealed off from everyone else with just Rachael, I'd do it in a heartbeat.

No. I wouldn't. I couldn't now that I had MJ and Nadia.

That was the problem. That would always be the problem. Thinking like this was circular—it always ended up in the same place, right where I started with no answers.

"MJ," Gina said, "your sister told me you're going to school?"

MJ took a deep drink of water. "Yes. I'll finish after this semester."

"And then what?"

Like she didn't know Enzo's plan. "Then I..." MJ looked at me. "I don't know," he said. I didn't know if he'd changed his mind about trying his hand at running Rocha Enterprises for Enzo with me as his mentor to show the old man up, or if he wasn't sure he should confide that information to her.

"I told him he should develop this property into a golf course," Nadia said, beaming at her mother.

Maddie tapped her fork tines on her plate.

"That's a wonderful idea!" Gina said. "Why have all of this property if you're not going to do anything with it?"

"I don't think the kids want to do that," Mr. Simcoe said, always the voice of reason, even though I was encouraging MJ to do something with the land. The future would look a lot more secure for him and Maddie if he started investing in it.

"The kids?" Gina glanced down at Maddie. "Oh, I didn't realize the two of you were married."

"As good as," MJ said, and left it at that.

Maddie took his hand and then stood up. "Who wants Joan's delectable chocolate cake?"

Joan nudged Beck with her shoulder. "I do," he said, raising his hand. "A big piece, too. Huge."

I couldn't hold back my laughter. I would've never thought in a million years that he'd end up with the Dragon Lady, as he used to call Joan. But they seemed to be pretty well matched.

"Who would've thought it, huh?" Rachael whispered to me.

She always knew my mind, my Rachael. "Not me."

We all ended up with big chunks of cake. I had a feeling Maddie didn't want any left over. Nadia pushed hers to the side. "I'm on a diet," she said. The girl never ate.

I picked up a forkful and looked around the table to gauge reactions before I tasted it. Everyone else was doing the same. "Oh, come on!" Joan said. "Do it together. One, two, *three*!"

We all eased our forks into our mouths. I was pleasantly surprised. It wasn't the best cake I'd ever eaten, but it wasn't bad either. "It's good," I said.

"Thank you," Joan said. I hadn't seen her so proud of herself since the high tower project in Dubai four years ago. Who knew making a cake could give her this much satisfaction?

"Delicious," Beck said, and gave her a kiss with frosting on his lips.

Everyone laughed. Thank God the two of them were here.

After dessert, Rachael and Joan helped Maddie clear the table. Gina and Nadia didn't even offer. I wanted to say something, but didn't know if it was my place. I helped Mr. Simcoe upstairs to one of the guest bedrooms. He was staying for the rest of the week and wanted to take a nap.

"I know you're in a hard spot, son," he said, patting the bed beside him for me to sit and talk. "But I also know you're a sharp fella. Don't let your heart and muddled mind overrule what your gut is telling you is right."

"What do you mean?" I asked, sinking down next to him.

"These women. When the day's said and done and you're an old man like me, who will be there with you? That's all the answer you need."

Rachael. Rachael would be there. Would Nadia? "How do I know who won't be there, though, if I don't give them the chance?"

"It's not about you giving it. It's about them proving it. There's nothing you need to do to make them love and accept you. They either will or they won't. I know it's hard with daughters. We want them to think we hung the moon. I can only imagine how you're feeling having just met your girl, but you don't owe her anything but your love and that doesn't mean turning a blind eye to who she really is inside."

"But what about unconditional love for your kids? You know, accepting them warts and all." That was what a father was supposed to do, wasn't it?

"You can still love them and admit to their flaws. My daughter can be a terrible, stubborn beast. She gets that from me. It's part of who she is. I want to throttle her when she gets into one of her moods, but I still love her. Acceptance doesn't mean denial."

"Right. But what now?"

"Confront what needs confronting. I think you've been

chewing at the wrong end of this problem." He cocked a brow. He meant Rachael.

Damn it. "You're right as always. I can talk to Rachael, so I ended up pinning everything on her, trying to fix it." I ran a hand over my head. "Shit."

He patted my back. "She loves you. She understands. She knows you can be a bullheaded moron at times, too."

"Got that right." I groaned and stood up. "Thank you. You always know just how to give me the kick in the ass I need."

"Anytime."

As I was leaving the room, he called to me. "Hey," he said, "tell Maddie to save me some of that cake."

"Not if I eat the last of it first."

I heard him chuckling as the door clicked shut.

Back home at Turtle Tear, I needed to get Rachael alone to talk, to apologize for being a bullheaded moron as Mr. Simcoe put it.

The cake might have been good, but it sat in our stomachs like rocks. Rachael, Gina, and I collapsed onto the leather sofas in the lounge as soon as we got inside. Nadia, cake-free and happy as a clam, strolled around the room picking up magazines and knickknacks. "I should call Paul," she said absentmindedly.

"What's that silver cup on the mantel?" Gina asked. "It's very old, isn't it?"

Nadia picked up Ingrid Weston's cup, the original matron of the hotel, and Rachael was off the couch like lightning. She didn't tear it out of Nadia's hands, but I knew she wanted to. The cup was very special to Rachael, who felt a close bond with the dead woman who used to live here.

"It belonged to the original owner of this island and hotel," she said, hovering.

"Let me see it," Gina said, reaching out to Nadia to take the cup.

Rachael was itching to take it back. I could sense her anxiety. But it was a silver cup. They weren't going to steal it or break it. "Why don't you tell them where we found it," I suggested to her.

Gina took it and ran her finger over the intricate engravings.

"It was in a trunk with a bunch of other antiques that belonged to Ingrid, the woman who lived here. We found them at the Weston Plantation. That was where her husband's family lived and where she died."

"Interesting," Gina said, barely listening. "What's this etching on the side?" She lifted it up by the lamp. "Oh my. These names. These are names in my family tree! It says: 'To Martha Ellen Border from E.M.' That's Evan Montgomery, her husband! My great-great-grandfather!"

"What?" Rachael said, her chin dropping in awe.

"We're related to the family who owned the Weston Plantation?" Nadia said, victory written all over her face.

"Well, who was Martha Ellen to Ingrid?" Gina asked Rachael.

"One of her husband's cousins."

"Wow," Nadia cried, bouncing on her toes, "we're descendants of the people who lived on the Weston Plantation and Turtle Tear!"

"Through marriage," Gina said, "yes."

Rachael was about to have a breakdown. "That is something," I said, standing and taking the cup from Gina, pretending I wanted to look at it, but really just wanting to place it back on the mantel and get it out of her hands. "If it's the same Montgomery family. That's a pretty common name, though."

"Not many with a Martha Ellen Border in the same family tree, though," Gina said, triumphant.

"No, I suppose not." I sat the cup back on the mantel.

"I'm going to go up and read for a while," Rachael said. "Let this cake digest." She tried to let out a laugh, but it sounded strangled.

"I'll be up in a bit," I said. "Think I'm going to take the Harley for a spin around the island first."

"Okay."

It was only six o'clock, but I knew she was going upstairs for the duration of the night. My guests were making her feel like a hostage in her own home.

"You have a Harley?" Gina asked once Rachael was out of the room.

"Just got it," I said, angling for the door.

"Oh, Dad! Take Mom for a ride," Nadia gushed. She

grasped Gina's arm. "You'll love it. He took me the other day. It was so much fun!"

"I do love motorcycles," Gina said. "They make you feel so alive." She stood up and followed me out to the patio, like I'd agreed to take her for a spin around the island. Our last trip hadn't ended so well.

"I only have one helmet," I said, doing my best to dissuade her without coming right out and being a jerk about it.

"That's okay. I trust you."

Great.

She got in the golf cart and rode with me to the boathouse. I didn't think her white capri pants or jewel-studded sandals where exactly the right attire for a motorcycle ride, but whatever. I'd just get it over with.

I straddled the bike and helped her on behind me. The engine was loud enough to wake the dead, so thankfully, we wouldn't have to talk. I headed out toward the gazebo and throttled the engine through the high grass. She held on tight around my waist and let out a "Woohoo!" in my ear.

I wanted to laugh. She was so proper and dressed so expensive all the time, but here was the girl I used to know. The fifteen-year-old was shining through out in the open air on the back of my bike. Maybe I could get somewhere with her once she cracked out of that fake shell.

When the gazebo came in to view, she patted my pack and pointed to it. I stopped and let the engine idle while she looked it over. "I want off!" she yelled.

Of course, why not prolong this? I turned the bike off

and helped her down. She jogged over to the gazebo and up the three steps, turning a circle right in its center. "This is beautiful, Merrick!"

"Beck built it." I slowly made my way over to the gazebo and leaned against the railing.

"This would be the perfect place for a wedding."

Weddings were not the topic of choice right now. "We had a fiftieth anniversary vow renewal ceremony for a couple here a few months back. Their whole family came for the weekend. It was really something."

I picked a long blade of grass and twisted it. She slowly walked over to me and put a hand on my arm. "I'm sorry. You're right. I owe you an apology. I was young and didn't know what to do. When I was old enough to break free from Enzo..." She took a shaky breath. "Well, you don't break free of Enzo, do you?"

I swallowed hard. "No. You don't. I'm sorry, too, Gina. It's my fault any of this happened. If I would've just kept it in my pants—"

"Then we wouldn't have MJ and Nadia." She leaned against my shoulder. "And it takes two. In case you forgot, I was the one who initiated it."

I let out a nervous laugh and stepped away. "Actually, I don't remember a lot about that encounter. Do you?"

She looked stricken. "Of course I do."

"Well," I backtracked, "I mean, I do, just not details. It was a long time ago and I was way too young to be doing it in the first place."

"Yeah." She sat on the step. So much for getting moving again. "I've always wondered what would've happened if I would've said no to disappearing. If I would've stayed and you had known about the babies."

"Gina, I was barely a teenager when they were born. We could hardly have gotten married or played house together." Where the hell was this heading?

"No. I know. I just mean, maybe when we were older, things could've been different. We might have wanted to try to make it work."

Sirens blared in my head. A voice screamed, *Abort! Abort!* This mission had gone terribly wrong. "I don't know."

"Is it so hard to imagine? My parents were in the same social circle as your father. If he hadn't paid my parents to send me away, we probably would've had the same friends. I bet it would've happened."

"Gina..." I shook my head. "It doesn't matter. We're here now. There's no going back."

"Isn't there?" She stood up and sauntered over to me. "I wonder what it would be like now...if we were together. If I seduced you like I did back then." She ran a fingernail down my jaw and under my chin.

"Don't," I said, catching her by the wrist. "I'm with Rachael. We're getting married."

"Are you sure?" She tilted her head and kissed my neck.

I jerked back. "Let's get going. This is over."

Gina took my hand. "It's not too late. You're not married

yet. We could try to make our family work." She played with my fingers. I gritted my teeth. "Nadia wants this so badly. She's always been a dreamer. MJ would be more accepting of me if you were more accepting. I want our kids to be happy, Merrick. I want to be part of their lives with you. We'll be grandparents someday. We could take family trips to Disney World and spoil our grandkids rotten, rock them to sleep when they spend the night. Take them out for ice cream on Sunday evenings. Doesn't that sound like fun?"

This was mind-blowing. It really seemed like she was being sincere. I would have to crush her and Nadia. She was right about MJ, too. He'd be more accepting of her if I was. I'd rob her of that as well.

Why did this woman have to come into my life now? If she'd proposed this before I met Rachael, I would've probably given it a shot. It would be the least I could do. She was the mother of my kids after all. If I were single, what would I have to lose? But now, there was Rachael, and there was no going back from Rachael.

"It's not going to happen, Gina. I'm sorry."

She let out a little snort of laughter. "Well, when you come to your senses and realize that your wife—if you get that far—is never going to accept your daughter and vice versa and that drives a wedge so far between the two of you that there's no alternative but to call it quits, you'll know where to find me."

"Is this what you want, or what Nadia wants? Is she

trying to come between Rachael and me intentionally?" Before she could answer, I held up a hand. "You know what? It doesn't matter. It won't work."

I turned and strode back to the bike, got on, and waited for her to get behind me. When she was on and holding tight, I took off. Her hands stroked my chest and my stomach. She pressed her breasts into my back. This woman was unbelievable.

Instead of going all the way around the island, I stopped back at the hotel. I'd take the bike back to the boathouse later. This ride was over.

Without a word, I got off and bolted toward the door into the lounge. I wanted that woman off this island and had to find a way to make her leave.

Nadia was answering her cell phone when I walked in. I waved to get her attention and tell her I was going upstairs when her face went pale, she let out a shriek and dropped her phone.

"No!" she cried.

I ran to her and took her in my arms. "What? What happened?"

She looked up at me with wide, horrified eyes. "He's dead."

Twenty-Eight

Rachael

Nadia cried out, sending me straight up in bed. I put my book down and hustled out of the bedroom and down the stairs. She sat on the sofa sobbing in Merrick's arms. Gina knelt in front of her holding her hand. It was a touching scene—for a mother, father, and daughter.

I leaned in the doorway and stayed out of their way.

Nadia took great, shaky breaths trying to calm down enough to speak. Finally, after Gina's coos and hair stroking, she collected herself enough to tell them what was going on.

"Paul?" Merrick asked.

She shook her head. "Grandfather. Enzo. He's dead!"

The shock of her words hit me as she broke into a sobbing fit again. Frozen where I stood, I watched Gina sink to the floor, hold her head in her hands, and begin to cry. "No," she sobbed, "it can't be true. No!"

Merrick, the only calm one among us, took Nadia by the shoulders. "Who was on the phone?"

"The housekeeper in Spain. Enzo has a villa there. She found him this morning. She tried to call Mom first. They think it was an aneurysm, but they want to do an autopsy."

Gina let out a howl like a dying cat. I felt terrible for her—for anyone who suffered a loss like this. Merrick sat Nadia back against the cushions and helped Gina to the sofa beside her. As he stood, his eyes found me.

"I'll get hot tea or something," I said, and turned for the kitchen.

I was taking tea bags out of the drawer when he came in. We just stared at each other. "Are you okay?" I asked.

"It—" He shrugged. "I don't know what to think."

He looked so lost. I went to him and took him in my arms. "No matter what went on between the two of you, he was your father. You can be upset, you know."

He kissed the top of my head. "I know. It hasn't hit me yet. How do I know it's really true? After all he's done—"

"It wouldn't be below him to fake his own death. I know." I hated what I was about to suggest, but it was all I could think of that might ease his mind. "Do you want to go over and see him before the burial?"

"No." He shook his head hard. "Absolutely not. Gina, Nadia, and my sister can go and handle everything."

"Okay."

A chapter was finally closed, but Enzo's death left loose ends. Gina and Nadia. I was certain he'd left them set financially, so that wasn't a concern, but would they go back to Europe now that the man who had been controlling their lives was gone?

"I better fix the tea," I said, pulling away. "Do you know what will happen to the Rocha Estate?" The big Tudor house outside Atlanta was where Merrick grew up. He'd been back only once as an adult.

"I don't know. Someone should tell Mr. Simcoe, Maddie, and MJ." He leaned against the counter and rubbed a hand over his head.

"I'll call. You take the tea in and keep Nadia and Gina calm." I poured the hot water over the tea bags in three mugs. "I'm sure Beck will fly them over as soon as they hear."

He blinked a few times, bewildered, still taking everything in. "Thank you."

"You don't have to thank me." I stroked his cheek. "I love you."

He took my hand and kissed my palm. "I love you, too."

I didn't want to leave him, but knew he had an obligation to be with Nadia right now, and given my rocky relationship with her, it wasn't the best time for me to intrude.

"I'll go upstairs and make the call." I rose up on my tiptoes, took his face in my hands, and kissed him. I wanted to convey so much in that kiss. That I was sorry, that he could depend on me, that I'd never leave him.

Upstairs, I stood in front of the open window beside the bed and dialed MJ's number. He answered on the third ring. "Hello?"

"MJ, it's Rachael. I have something to tell you."

"This doesn't sound good. What's wrong?"

"Everyone here is fine, but Nadia got a phone call a little while ago. Enzo's dead."

There was a pause. I wasn't sure he was still on the line. "MJ?"

"I'm here. Wow. I wasn't expecting that."

"It was sudden. He was in Spain. They're saying it was an aneurysm."

"How's Merrick taking it?"

"He's still processing it, I think." I rested my forehead against the windowpane and closed my eyes.

"I'll let Maddie and her dad know and ask Beck to fly us over."

"Okay."

"And Rachael? Thanks for being there for him through everything. I know having Nadia and Gina there has to be hard enough. Now this. He'd be lost without you."

"There's nowhere else I want to be." My chest swelled with hope. Hope that our future could get back on track.

"We'll see you soon."

As soon as Beck dropped off MJ, Maddie, and Mr. Simcoe, he was off again with Nadia and Gina.

Their departure was rushed, but Gina didn't miss her chance to kiss Merrick on the cheek and tell him she was sorry. Nadia hadn't stopped crying. Merrick held her tight and gently swayed back and forth like a parent does a small child to settle them. He kissed her forehead and helped them both into the helicopter before saying good-bye. Neither one of them said a word of good-bye to me. I didn't hold it against them due to their grief. I just hoped they never returned.

Beck clapped Merrick on the back. "I'll be back in a day or so, and we'll have a few beers."

Merrick, hands in pockets, shrugged. "I'm good, man."

"Yeah. I know you are." Beck climbed up in the helicopter, and the rest of us backed away so he could get the propellers going.

As they lifted off into the air, they took all my anxiety and doubt with them. My home, my island, my Merrick—they were all mine again.

Once we were back at the hotel, Merrick, MJ, Maddie, Mr. Simcoe, and I sat on the patio. "I hate to say it," Mr. Simcoe said, "but Enzo and I had some good times."

Maddie huffed. "Dad, he put you in the hospital. You didn't forget that, did you? It was only a couple months ago."

"No, I didn't forget. I choose to remember the good times, too, out of respect for the departed. We spent a lot of time on the golf course together."

"I don't have any good memories," MJ said. "He shipped me off to boarding school and spent summers annoyed that I had to be under his roof."

Merrick sat back in his chair with his arms crossed. "What about you?" I asked him. "Anything from when you were a kid that's a good memory?"

He sat there for a moment and didn't say anything. I

didn't think he would. Then he leaned forward and clasped his hands together. "He loved my mom. He wasn't an evil bastard until she died. That's all I can say for him."

"What about you?" MJ asked me. "You met him."

"What do I have to say about Enzo?" This was tricky. The man ruined the life of everyone he came across, made a game of it. But he was dead and nothing I could say would make a difference. "He kept a very organized office."

Merrick looked at me out of the corner of his eye, smirking before chuckling. "He kept an organized office."

The rest of them started laughing, and before I knew it, we were all holding our stomachs, cracking up. It was a dumb thing to say, but I was glad I said it for lack of anything else.

As night fell, we all took solace in our rooms. Merrick and I held each other under the soft, white sheet and watched the moon climb high in the sky through the window. We didn't speak, because there was nothing to say that couldn't wait. We were content, our problems not solved, but out of our line of sight for now. The time would come when we'd have to talk about us, when we'd have to face our future and what it looked like, but not tonight.

Twenty-Nine

Merrick

There was a heaviness I didn't expect to feel when my father died. I hated the man and that was no exaggeration. He'd ruined my life and wouldn't have stopped ruining it if he'd lived, so with that heaviness was a relief that was wrapped in guilt like some morbid gift from the dead.

I worried about Mr. Simcoe. He'd considered Enzo his best friend until recently. I don't think he'd come to terms with his former best friend physically assaulting him and now Enzo was dead. Mr. Simcoe was the type of man who needed to forgive and find resolution. He'd get none now.

Rachael would say I needed to find forgiveness and closure myself. She might be right, but there wasn't a way to do that. I couldn't say my piece to a dead man. There were so many questions I'd never get answers to. The biggest: Why did he hate me?

It didn't matter, though. I should've thanked him for being such a bastard. It taught me how not to be a father. To be the best dad I could be to MJ and Nadia, all I had to do was the exact opposite of what my father would do. I wanted to encourage them and help them, always be there and believe in their dreams.

Someday I hoped there would be more kids to be a good dad to, to see grow from infants to little kids, teenagers into adults.

Enzo's autopsy came back conclusive of an aneurysm. He'd gone out of this world as he should have: alone and suffering. I'd called Nadia every day in the week since his death. She was coping and over the initial shock of the news. She and Gina were staying on in Spain until Enzo's will was read, which was to take place this afternoon. They asked me to attend, but it seemed unlikely that I'd get the properties back he'd bought out from under me, so I elected to say where I belonged on Turtle Tear. MJ outright refused to go. He, Maddie, Beck, and Joan were flying in anytime now.

From where I lay in the hammock under the pool cloister, I could just make out Rachael in the distance talking with a man from a company that installed zip lines. She'd booked her first corporate outing on the island, and they were looking for team-building activities. Never one to disappoint, Rachael was rising to the challenge.

I needed to talk to her, but I was afraid of pushing. I told her we'd postpone the wedding until she came to terms with the new dynamics of my life with Nadia and Gina—who I hoped stayed in Spain for the rest of her life. I'd already gone against my plan and proposed too soon. I couldn't let my gut talk me into something I knew in my head was wrong. She needed time and she wasn't going anywhere. I could make myself sit back and wait.

Not that it was easy. We walked around like nothing stood between us, ignoring the giant lingering in the shadows. I had a feeling Rachael was waiting for me to initiate another conversation, but we were both stubborn and at a standstill until one of us gave in.

When I heard the helicopter approaching, I got off the hammock and fired up the Harley to get me to the landing pad. Rachael glanced over and I waved, letting her know I was on my way to meet everyone.

The day was humid and overcast, pressure burgeoning in the clouds. By nightfall, a storm would set in over the island. I was glad Beck got them here before it hit.

I rounded a corner in the path and pulled ahead of the trees. The helicopter was in full view, descending, blowing the tall grass flat.

It wasn't Beck. It was the helicopter Gina had arrived in. What the hell was she doing back?

I pulled to the side and killed the bike's engine. Once the copter was on the ground and the propellers stopped, the pilot climbed out. He lifted a hand and strode toward me. Looking closer, I didn't see anyone else flying with him.

I met him halfway. "Hello, Mr. Rocha," he said, and extended his hand, holding an envelope. "From Ms. Montgomery."

If I could've refused it, I would've. Instead, I took it. "Thanks."

"She says to read it in private." He nodded and turned, heading back to his bird.

It had to be news from Enzo's will.

I wanted to burn it and never know what it said inside.

I folded the envelope in half, tucked it in my back pocket, and cranked the throttle on the bike, eager to blow off some steam.

Beck landed at a little after six in the evening when I was in the boathouse polishing the Harley. I helped the five of them drag themselves and their suitcases into the hotel. MJ was in a mood and I could tell it was affecting all of them.

Mr. Simcoe immediately took off to examine his flower beds, rose pruners in hand. "He's been driving the landscapers crazy," Maddie said irritably, plopping down at the kitchen table.

Rachael came bustling into the kitchen and hugged MJ. "I'm sorry for your loss," she said.

He turned away, face shadowed by his dark temper. "I didn't lose anything."

She looked at me and tilted her head toward him as if to say, *Talk to him*.

I knew he was hurting even if the old man had treated him like shit. Enzo raised him—if you call shuttling him off to boarding schools raising him.

I put a hand on Beck's shoulder. "How about that beer now? MJ, have a cold one with us."

MJ leaned against the counter. "Yeah. Sure. Whatever."

Joan beat me to the fridge and handed me the beer bottles. "Good luck," she whispered. "For what it's worth, I think karma did the bastard in." She strode away, over to the table, to sit beside Maddie. I was glad she didn't wait for a reply, because really, what was there to say? Joan had always been pretty perceptive.

I ran a hand down Rachael's back as I walked past her and headed out to the patio with Beck and MJ. With the man she loathed dead and the two women she wanted gone, gone, I left her to a proper celebratory chat with Joan and Maddie. I could only imagine that conversation.

Leaning back in my chair, I cracked open my beer and took a long pull from the bottle. It burned going down it was so cold, but it went down easy. I had a feeling before this night was over, I'd kill a few of these soldiers.

Beck looked relaxed sitting there between MJ and me. I swear, nothing could rattle him. Not even death. MJ held his bottle on the table like it might escape, picking the label with his thumbnail. "Conflicted?" I asked.

He raised his eyes to me. "What?"

"I said, are you conflicted? I am. The man was a fucking asshole. I hated him for most of my life. Still, he was the only father I had. Now he's dead. What am I supposed to do with that?"

MJ let out a snort of derision. "Yeah. What the fuck do you do with that?"

"So you feel me then," I said, and took another long drink from my bottle.

He tipped his own back and drank. "Yeah," he said, "I feel ya."

"Glad we're in this together." I reached across and tapped the neck of his bottle with mine. Enzo took everything I had, but he was dead and gone and I still had MJ and Beck, Rachael, Turtle Tear, Nadia. I had my friends, my family, and my home. Enzo's reign of terror had been broken.

"You two sorry saps about done crying in your beer?" Beck asked, propping one foot up on his opposite knee. "Or are we going to drink to the fact that the man who took everything away from you, Merrick, including your son and daughter, is dead? I, for one, will be happy to spit out a big old loogie on his grave."

MJ chuckled. "I won't stop you."

"Like you could, Junior. Where are they burying him anyway? Might want to get some voodoo priestess in on that shit. Keep him from roaming around haunting people."

"Not sure, but now is as good a time as any to find out." I pulled the envelope from my back pocket. "Gina sent this earlier today. I haven't opened it yet."

"No time like the present," Beck said, sitting forward.

Like me, MJ eyed the letter like there might be a viper tucked inside ready to strike as soon as I unsealed the flap. He felt me, all right. We were of one mind.

I took a deep breath and groaned as I exhaled, ripping the end of the envelope open. Inside there were four pages folded together. On top of the first page I read the words: *Last Will and Testament.* "No," I whispered. "Why did she send me this?"

"What is it?" MJ asked, staring at me like he didn't really want to know.

"A copy of Enzo's will. At least part of it." I flipped through the pages. One section was highlighted. There was a sticky note stuck to the page right under the highlighted section. *I'm sorry* was written in feminine handwriting.

I put the other three pages down on the table and focused on the emphasized sentences.

I read them once. The message didn't register. What was this telling me?

I read them twice. No. It couldn't be true. Nobody would do that.

I read them a third time and felt my heart stop beating in my chest for a moment. "Jesus. No."

My hand holding the page dropped to my lap. I stared at MJ across the table. It couldn't be true. But it was. I knew it was. Not because it said so in Enzo's will, but because I felt it in my soul to be the truth.

"What is it?" MJ asked, brows creased in concern.

"You." I held up the paper and shook my head.

"What do you mean, me?"

"You're not my son. You're my brother."

"What?" He bolted from his chair and snatched the

paper from my hand. I watched as his eyes scanned over the same section mine had, not once, or twice, but three times. "I don't—why? How?"

I dropped my head into my hands. It was unbelievable. "They set me up. Dad was screwing the babysitter, knocked her up, and they pinned it on me. Shit. No wonder I don't remember much about being with her. Other than the fact that I was too young to know what the hell I was doing—I... Jesus. I didn't get her pregnant."

Beck stood up and started pacing. "This is fucking crazy. I mean like soap opera crazy. This doesn't happen in real life."

MJ read the page again, shaking his head. "He was my father? The whole time. He didn't want me around. Talked to me like I was a piece of shit. I was his son." He wadded up the page and slammed it on the table. *"I was his fucking son!"*

A second later, Maddie came running out, followed by Rachael and Joan. Maddie took one look at MJ and me, and panic spread across her face. "What's wrong?"

Beck took Joan by the arm and hauled her back inside. I held my hand out to Rachael. "Enzo left us a confession in his will."

I felt my heart cracking. I didn't lose MJ, but he wasn't my son. I'd come to terms with him as my own and took pride in having him call me Dad. Now I find out it was another lie. Rachael looked right through me. She saw the hurt. It reflected on her own face. "What?" she whispered, already horrified by what she didn't know.

"I'm not his son," MJ said, pissed. "We're brothers."

"What?" Maddie gripped MJ's arms. "What do you mean, brothers?"

"I mean, Enzo was my father. He was the one who got Gina pregnant." His fists were clenched and his face was red. He wanted to punch something. I'd had that feeling more times in my life than I could count. But not now. Right now I wanted to cry.

"So," Rachael said, stunned, "he's your brother and Nadia's your sister?"

It was the wrong time to say it. "Yeah, you're rid of her. Congratulations. You don't have to be a stepmom after all." I flung the words at her and saw them hit, like a physical blow. I couldn't help it. I'd lost a son—even if I did gain a brother—and the first thing she says has to do with Nadia not being mine as well? It got right under my skin and dug in deep.

"That's not what I meant," she said, but her hopeful tone when she'd said it told me otherwise.

She picked up the rest of the pages and scanned through them. Her eyes got wide, blinking double time. "Did you bother to read the rest of this?"

"No. I kind of stopped at the highlighted section and hadn't gotten passed it yet."

She shoved the pages into my chest. "You have one fourth of your properties back. Gina, Nadia, and MJ get the other three fourths. *And* he wants his ashes sprinkled here. By you."

"What?" Disbelieving, I grasped the papers and read for myself. I didn't care about the properties. I'd resigned myself to being without my company. But why would he want me to spread his ashes here? "I don't get it. It doesn't make sense."

"One last way to control you," MJ said. "To make you do something you don't want to do. He'll be here with you after death."

"You can't do it," Maddie said, both hands to her face, fingers pressed to her lips.

"He has to." Rachael crossed her arms and held my eyes with hers. "It's the only way to let go. He doesn't have control. Just because he requested something in his will doesn't mean you have to do it."

"And how does doing what he wants give me control?" For the first time ever, I was suffering and it felt like she didn't understand me. Rachael always understood me. I didn't need this on top of the shit pile I'd been served.

"You're doing it on your terms, knowing you don't have to and that there are no consequences if you don't. If you do it, it's because you're able to face this last challenge he's given you. If you don't, he's still able to get inside you and you let him win."

I couldn't even think. In the span of fifteen minutes, Enzo Rocha had once again flipped my world on its head. He'd lied all this time about Gina, about MJ and Nadia, to protect himself. He'd had sex with a minor and gotten her pregnant. When she wouldn't give it up, he paid off her family and talked them all into pretending she was dead along with Nadia, then passed MJ off as his grandson.

The deviousness...The insanity...I couldn't breathe around it. "I have to think," I said. "I'll be back." I rounded the table and hooked an arm around MJ's neck, pulling him into me. "This changes nothing, brother." He hugged me back.

I glanced at Rachael before I pushed the patio gate open. She was my strength, but lately she didn't have strength to give because of Nadia. That situation still sat like a huge rock in the middle of a stream, dividing us. It didn't have to now, but there was the lingering question of how much she'd sacrifice to be with me. I'd give her the world if she asked. Lay down and die in a second for her. Would she have done the same for me?

Her eyes were wet and she wiped at the corner of one before looking down. We needed to talk, to straighten *us* out.

It would have to wait a little longer. I was suffocating. Time and space, solitude, that was what I needed. The rest would have to settle on the back burner for a while.

Thirty

Rachael

Merrick was devastated and so was I. If he thought Enzo's confession hadn't affected me, he was wrong and had misjudged all the time we'd spent together. Did he not trust that I loved him? That I loved MJ? That this would shake me up, too?

One problem with being on a small island was finding a place to be alone. I knew where Merrick had most likely gone—the tree house. It killed me that he could be there without me. That he hadn't come to me when he needed comfort. The relationship between Nadia and me had given him reason to doubt me.

I sat in the orchard under a tree, twisting my engagement ring around my finger.

How had we gotten so lost?

After an hour crying and brooding, it hit me. If I wanted him to know I would stand beside him no matter what, I had to go to him. I couldn't let him walk away. I knew in my gut—in my heart and soul—that he needed me right now, but here I was, crying in self-pity on the ground.

If the tables were turned, he'd be with me no matter what.

I raced across the lawn and into the trees to the path that led to the tree house. Rain had started to fall, one lazy drop after another. Tears from the sky. They fell on my skin, dripping from the leaves above, and ran down my arms and legs.

The tree house was dark. He hadn't turned any lights on, but I knew he was inside.

I dashed up the steps to the deck. The door was ajar. I paused with my hand on the knob for a moment to catch my breath before pushing it open and striding inside.

Looking around the cool darkness of the main room, I saw no sign of him. Then my eye caught the thick, round pillar candle sitting on the bottom step of the spiral staircase, lit.

The Nelsons had sent it to us after celebrating their fiftieth anniversary by renewing their vows here. They said we reminded them of themselves at our age. The candle was the unity candle they lit at their wedding. The minister told them to set it out and light it whenever one of them needed to talk with the other.

And here it was, burning on the bottom step. Merrick reaching out. He had faith that I'd come to him after all.

I picked up the candle and carried it up the stairs to the big bedroom at the top. Merrick was lying on his stomach on the bed, head turned away, arms bent underneath the pillow. I set the candle on the dresser and went to him.

The bed lowered as I sat on it. I put a hand on his back. There was so much to say, but at the same time, nothing I could say would be right. "I'm sorry" was useless. He'd gained a son and daughter and lost them—not gone, but not who he thought they were. He'd lived a lifetime of regret for something that never happened. He'd been victimized by the man who should've protected him, but chose to save his own skin instead.

Words were ash in the wind.

I lay beside him and pressed close, stroking his hair and kissing his shoulder. He rolled to his side and looked at me. His eyes ran over my hair and face, down my neck, and over my shoulders. He grasped my hips and pulled me even closer. "I've been losing you, too," he whispered, striking me like lightning to the chest.

"No. Never." I held his face in my hands and kissed him hard. "Never, Merrick."

"All that with Nadia. So much wasted time arguing and she was never mine to begin with." He shook his head and took my hands from his face. "You couldn't deal with it, though. What happens when something else comes crashing into our lives? What if you can't take it?"

"I could take it. You *need* to listen to me and believe what I tell you. She knew all along, Merrick. She and Gina were playing their part in Enzo's plan. She wanted you to build Rocha back up, marry Gina, and the two of them would have access to everything."

His face was so somber, it killed me. "How did you know?" he said. "You doubted me and what I believed to be one hundred percent true. You saw them playing me for a fool."

I sat up and looked down at him. "Merrick Enzo Rocha. If you ever thought I was the type of woman to go along blindly with whatever crazy idea popped into your head, I'm not sure how you ever came to that conclusion. I will fight you every step of the way," I said, poking him in the chest, "if I think you're doing something stupid. It doesn't mean I don't believe in you. It means I will look out for you. You're part of me. I won't go along with something that I believe will hurt you."

He grabbed my finger. "What if Nadia had been mine? How would you have accepted it?"

"I tried with her, Merrick. She was on a mission. Eventually, the truth would've come out. In the meantime, I would've kept trying. For you. Because I love you and I'll do anything for you. You believe that, don't you?"

He cupped my cheek. "I doubted it, Rachael. I can't lie to you about that."

I squeezed his wrist. "*Never* doubt that. It was hard—almost impossible—to watch you trust her over me."

"I—"

"No. You did. You took her side and believed I was the bad guy, Merrick. I get it. You thought she was your daughter, a daughter who spent twenty years without you. You felt guilty and would've spent the rest of your life trying to make it up to her if the truth hadn't come out."

He clamped his lips, frowning. I ran my hands up his chest. "We were tested," I said. "Hard. We nearly failed. Now we learn from it and move forward. We believe in each other no matter what, even if what the other thinks seems impossible to believe. We do it. It's the only way."

He nodded, reached for me, and pulled me down on his chest. "We'll never be one mind," I said, snuggling in, "but we need to compromise and understand each other."

Merrick ran his fingers through my hair. "I promised you when we got engaged to be better about communicating. I haven't been."

"You had a long way to come. It's not like you had a family to show you how it's done." I lifted my head and propped my chin on his chest. "Don't worry. I'll show you. Even if I have to beat it into your thick skull."

He smiled and I touched my lips to his lightly, a grin of my own matching his. "There's only one more question then," he said, wrapping his arms tightly around my waist. "Do you still want to marry me the Saturday after Thanksgiving?"

I knocked on his head. "Sometimes you can be so dense. I never *didn't* want to marry you the Saturday after Thanksgiving."

He chuckled, then gave me a sorrowful expression. "I'm sorry about your grandma's dress."

I traced my finger along his jawline. "I haven't heard if Mom was able to find someone who could get the stain out. There's still hope."

"I'll keep my fingers crossed." He rolled me over to my back and ran his hand up my sundress. "When they're not in use, that is." He lowered his head and kissed me, soft and slow, gliding his tongue along my bottom lip. "Are we good?" he whispered.

"We've been good since the day I woke up on this island in your bed."

Merrick's black eyes went dark and sexy. "Best thing I ever did was keep you in my bed."

"Hmm. I believe the determination was mine. I kept you in *my* bed, Mr. Rocha."

He grabbed my wrists and pinned them above me. "Now you'll spend the rest of your nights in *our* bed, soon-to-be Mrs. Rocha."

The sound of his deep voice saying "Mrs. Rocha" sent a thrill through my body. God, I could not wait.

His mouth skimmed my neck as his hands pushed my dress up. "I want this off. Now." I sat up and he yanked it over my head and threw it across the room. "I suck at explaining myself with words, so I'm going to tell you how much I love and want you the best way I know how."

In an instant, I was naked and he was settling my legs over his shoulders. "When I'm not with you every night, I miss your taste on my tongue." His mouth dove between my legs, his tongue wet and warm, spreading me open.

"When my hands aren't on you," he said, his breath hot against my sensitive flesh, his finger pushing inside me, "or in you, I miss how you feel." His other hand slid up my body and cupped my breast, squeezing and toying with my nipple.

He stayed quiet, his mouth too busy to speak, so

I did the talking. "I love grabbing on to your hair when you're between my legs." I threaded my fingers in his thick locks and tugged gently as he sucked and licked, guiding him where I needed him and pressing his mouth harder against me.

I squirmed and rotated my hips, the hot, tingling sensation growing to a prickling ache for release. I dug my heels into his back and bucked my pelvis. So close. "I'm going to—oh God—yes, yes—"

He pulled his lips away and looked up at me. "What I miss most is feeling you let go. In my mouth, around my fingers, clenching my cock." Then his mouth was back on me and I was pulling his hair and crying out, riding his mouth. I didn't think it would end. Didn't want it to end.

My eyes stayed closed. I felt him get up. When I opened them, he was stripping off his jeans; his chest was bare. He licked his lips and smiled. "Now comes what I love the most." He climbed back onto the bed, stopping on his knees between my legs. "Being inside you. Making love to you."

I clasped my ankles around his waist. "What if I want to be the one making love to you?"

He took my hands and brought them to his lips, kissing my knuckles as he pushed forward and eased inside me. "We'll make love to each other."

"Then come down here." I pulled his chest down against mine. "I want to feel your whole body." I ran my hands down his strong back and squeezed his perfect butt. My nipples grazed against his chest as he moved inside me.

"Keep your eyes on mine," he said. "I love seeing them haze over when you let go."

"Yours get even darker somehow," I told him. "And they flicker like fire."

He dropped his chin and flicked my nipple with his tongue. "Flicker, huh?"

I flicked my tongue across his earlobe. "Yeah," I whispered, before taking it between my lips.

His hands slid under my butt, lifting it, and his pace increased. I could feel every blessed inch of him, thick and hard, claiming me. If this wasn't Heaven, I didn't ever want to go there. "It's so good," I said, locking eyes with him again. "Every time. So good."

"I was made to fit inside you." He thrust and rolled his hips.

I moaned. "I was made to hold you inside me."

He rose up on his elbows and held my hands, our fingers entwined. "I won't ever lose this, Rachael. This is essential for me to keep breathing. You're my air. You keep me alive."

He thrust and I met each one. "You're my blood," I said, rising up to meet him. "My bones." I swiveled my hips in time with his, my breath coming faster, my muscles clenching around him. "My soul."

I squeezed his hands tight, the rush taking me again. "My heart," he groaned as I throbbed and contracted. "Merrick," I panted.

"My love." He dropped his forehead to my chest, stilled his body, and pulsed inside me.

We lay together for a long time, still connected, inhaling and exhaling at the same time, our heartbeats in sync. The sun went down and the candle on the dresser glowed, sending a halo of warm light across the wall.

We'd been through so much together in such a short time. It felt like years had passed between us, but it was only the beginning. There was a lifetime left to be lived.

A giddiness passed through me. Having Merrick was a gift. A dream come true.

I couldn't wait to be his wife.

Thirty-One

Merrick

Enzo's ashes came a week later in a plastic container, delivered by the same pilot who'd dropped off the copy of the will, and we got them settled in their final resting place that same afternoon.

Mr. Simcoe captained the boat. Maddie and Rachael stood to the side as MJ and I took turns dumping his ashes into the murky Everglades swamp water.

"Our Father, who art in Heaven," Mr. Simcoe began to recite. The rest of us joined in.

The honor and irony of disposing of my father's remains settled heavily in my bones. I'd wanted him out of my life for as long as I could remember.

Now he was.

Watching the white-gray ash blow on the wind and float on the water was freeing, but at the same time, unsettling. I'd never know why he did it. I mean, he'd done it to save his own ass. That I got. But how could a man do that to his son? I'd already lost my mother.

This wasn't the closure I'd expected it to be.

Rachael took my hand. "It'll take time to say good-bye, but you will. Eventually, the hurt will stop."

She knew my heart and mind so well. "I hope so."

She nodded and kissed my cheek. "You'll let it all go."

I had a plan. My brother, MJ, was in on it. Rachael would get the wedding she wanted whether she knew it or not. There wasn't much time to pull it off, only a couple months. In the meantime, Rachael, Maddie, and Joan put together a guest list.

Joan was a huge help. I had to admit, I never thought I'd see the day she and Rachael were friends, but seeing them sitting at the big farmhouse table in the kitchen at the Weston Plantation, there was no denying it.

Mr. Simcoe sat across the table with Maddie, flipping through an old book of plants and flowers. Rachael wanted to carry something native to the area down the aisle to complement her calla lilies, and my old-fashioned girl would get to wear her grandmother's dress after all.

My soon-to-be mother-in-law was a genius. She hired a seamstress to sew a layer of lace over the bodice to hide the stain. I wouldn't get to see it before the ceremony, but I heard all about it after Rachael was done squealing with delight on the phone the day before.

MJ and I, with Beck's help, had some heroic feats to pull off before the big day. Rachael's plan to go home for a bridal shower the weekend before would help. There were a lot of people to contact while she was gone and a lot of unplanning all of her hard work.

In the end, she'd be so surprised and happy. I couldn't wait to see her face.

There was a second surprise I had in mind for her, but it took calling Paul Renault. I'd been reluctant, unsure what he knew about our family situation and if he still spoke with Nadia. It turned out they weren't in touch and he'd started seeing another woman.

I congratulated him before getting down to business. The details had to be finalized, but my wedding gift to Rachael was going to be a dream for her.

Having her in my life was a dream to me.

MJ came into the kitchen, where I was leaning against the counter drinking coffee and watching the plans come together. He handed me a check.

"What's this?" I asked.

"I got an inheritance from Enzo. I'm paying you back for this place." He leaned beside me.

I tore up the check. "Not going to happen."

"You're not my father, Merrick. I have the money. I want you to take it."

"Not the point." I took a sip of coffee. Its heat settled in my stomach. "I thought you were my son. I bought you this place. I don't care if you're my brother or my cousin or my uncle. You're family. I gave it to you as a gift and don't want your money."

He was nearly thirteen years younger than me and had never had someone to look out for him. I'd be that guy. I'd taken that on and I wasn't planning on quitting. "Call it a graduation present from your big brother if you have to," I said.

"Quite a gift," he said, grabbing a coffee mug out of the cupboard.

His finals were a week after the wedding. I knew the stress he'd be under trying to pull off my scheme and getting ready to pass his exams for graduation. "I owe you."

His eyes roamed across the room to the table, where the planning and chatter were endless. "Yeah, you do." He chuckled.

Beck came in and stood behind Joan, his hands on her shoulders. He bent and kissed the top of her head. I didn't care what he said. His actions spoke for him.

The kitchen was warm. Not the warm you get from a hot autumn day, but the warmth that only comes from family. I was surrounded by family. These people would be in my life for a long time to come. They'd fill my home, my holidays, and be there when our family grew. We'd be parents and grandparents together. We'd see each other through the hard times and celebrate the good ones.

It was amazing how one year could change your life. Where I'd once had nothing, nobody, I now had a home and a family. All it took was one woman and one crazy night when I whisked her away to Turtle Tear.

The night I took my Rachael, I gave my heart to her completely.

There was something almost poetic about that.

Something I'd vow to cherish for the rest of our lives.

Read the book that started the erotic journey of a lifetime . . .

Please see the next page for an excerpt from

Taken

Prologue

My fingers shake as I log onto the video chat. I can't believe I've made it this far into the interview process with Rocha Enterprises. This is my dream job, and a shot at being the project manager for the renovation of historic Turtle Tear Hotel working for a world-renowned company. It's a bigger opportunity than I ever imagined I'd have.

I've researched Turtle Tear Island and the background of the hotel extensively. There's no way anyone else is a better candidate for the position, and the fact that I made it this far—through the basic human resources interviews to an interview with the CEO himself—is proof of that.

I click my mouse to connect. I'm five minutes early, but my interviewer is already logged into the video chat. My palms become slick with sweat, and I wipe them on my pants.

"Hello, Ms. DeSalvo. I see you're prepared to start early."

Even with my cheap webcam displaying a grainy image, the warm smile greeting me from the screen should put me at ease, but I'm intimidated as all hell. Maybe it's the deep voice that sends prickles of heat down my neck and flushes my cheeks, or the handsome, clean-shaven face. It could be the tidy, slicked back hair that makes this feel so intimidating and all too real.

This can't possibly be real. I have to be dreaming.

The dark, piercing eyes on my monitor are most definitely dreamy.

What am I thinking? This is an interview with the CEO of Rocha Enterprises, not some dating website meet and greet. I have to pull myself together.

"Hello." My voice cracks. I clear my throat, straighten my shoulders and smile. "I'm willing to bet I'm the most prepared applicant you've spoken to."

There. I exude confidence.

My boasting is rewarded with the flicker of an eyebrow and a repressed smirk. "Is that so?"

Oh, that voice sends goose bumps crawling up my arms.

"Maybe you can tell me something I don't know then. Go ahead and impress me, Ms. DeSalvo."

My mind flashes through the dozens of facts I know about the property. Despite my staunch desire to remain professional, my over-eager libido rears its head when my interviewer rubs a long finger over a full bottom lip. Somehow, I find myself reciting the romantic love story of Turtle Tear's founder and his wife instead of something more professionally relevant, like the ecological importance of preserving the integrity of the island.

"Did you know, Mr. Rocha, that Archibald Weston built the hotel to impress a woman?" I wait for a curious lift of the chin in response before I continue. "Mr. Weston was desperate to win the affections of Ingrid Burkhart. He convinced himself that building her a magnificent place to live would win her hand in marriage.

"Turtle Tear Island with its lush green trees and beautiful wild flowers seemed like the perfect place to build it. Archibald grew up in the area and paddled his canoe to the tranquil island every chance he had." I stop to take a breath and to make sure I'm not droning on too long and losing my audience.

That long finger glides across those amazing lips again. Instantly, I imagine how soft and firm they would feel pressed against my own. Why does my webcam image have to be so awful? If I get this job, I'm buying one that displays in high def.

"You're an excellent storyteller, Ms. DeSalvo." A trace of humor mingles with the deep timbre. Could this be a trifecta? Wealthy, good looking *and* a sense of humor? "I'm entranced. Please, continue."

"During the course of Archibald's business ventures, he'd visited the Yucatan and been taken with the Hacienda-style cattle ranches in the region. Turtle Tear Hotel was modeled after a ranch where he'd stayed during one of his visits."

"Is that so?" Those eyes and a strong jawline come closer to the screen.

My story is impressive. I'm nailing this interview.

"Yes, that is so. Anyway, he built Ingrid a grand hotel since the island is remote and he knew she would want friends and family to visit and stay. Once it was completed, he showed up on Ingrid's doorstep, dropped to one knee and instead of proposing, presented her with the deed for Turtle Tear Hotel."

I hear a low, exhaled, "Hmm..." and some shuffling of papers. My screen blurs with movement. "I'm just making notes. Please, go on."

I take a deep breath and squeeze my hands together. The next part is my favorite.

"Archibald told her he'd put his blood, sweat, tears, and entire heart into building the home where he wanted to spend the rest of his life, and since she owned his life, it was all hers to have. He only hoped she'd let him keep his soul, which was bound to hers for all eternity."

"Wow. That's an incredible declaration. He was a brave man."

My heart pounds. I'm afraid it can be seen beating against my blouse on the other side of the small camera. "Yes. He was very brave and entirely selfless in his pursuit of Ingrid."

"I assume she accepted since they were married?" The question comes through in a louder, more insistent tone that makes my speakers crackle. Something else to add to my wish list.

"Actually, no. She told him he needed her parents blessing if she was to return to Turtle Tear with him." I clear my throat and can't suppress a grin. "This is where the story gets really interesting."

"It gets *even better*?" My grin is reflected back on a pair of delicious-looking lips framed by deep dimples on both sides. The image pixelates and freezes.

"Much." I fiddle with my webcam cord trying in vain to get a better connection. "Archibald and Ingrid were the Romeo and Juliet of the Civil War. His family supplied sugar cane from their plantation to the Confederate troops. Ingrid's family housed Confederate deserters. Even though it was August 1865 and the war had ended, there was no way Ingrid's parents were going to give Archibald their blessing to marry their daughter and take her away."

"What did he do?"

Damn. I wish I could see the expression that accompanies the urgency conveyed in the tone of the question, but my screen is still frozen on that set of white teeth and pair of dimples. Not that I mind. I'm considering making it my new screensaver.

"He tried his best for months to convince her parents he was worthy of Ingrid, even offering to let them live at the hotel, too, but they wouldn't budge. Finally, heartbroken with nothing left to lose, he climbed a ladder up to her window one night, broke in, and whisked her away.

"Ingrid was furious at first, but when she got to Turtle Tear, it was love at first sight and she refused to ever leave the island again. It's said that she's buried there, but no grave marker has ever been found to confirm that fact."

I sit back in my chair—mirroring your interviewer was a tip I acquired in an interview workshop—and wait for a response.

"That's quite a big risk for the love of a woman. I supposed it paid off for him in the end. Would you agree, Ms. DeSalvo?"

"Yes. The lengths he went to just to win her over...I'm sorry. Ingrid and Archibald's story always overwhelms me." I put a hand to my chest and inhale deeply to catch my breath. "His grand, romantic gesture won him his wife and the home where he lived the rest of his life. I hope to work with your company to restore the property and hotel to its original style and design, to make it a place nobody would ever want to leave."

"Something Archibald and Ingrid would be proud of?"

My chest fills with emotion that can't be repressed. An enormous smile threatens to split my face in half. "I'd love nothing more, Mr. Rocha. Given the opportunity—"

"The opportunity is yours. I've never seen someone so passionate and knowledgeable about a rundown hotel on swamp land in the Everglades. I'd be a fool to entrust anyone less enthusiastic with this project. In fact, you're the only one I'd trust it to. Nobody has proven themselves more deserving."

The rest of the interview becomes a blur. A haze of details and names of H.R. personnel who will be in touch to discuss salary and relocation. My head is in the clouds. My dream realized.

I'm the newest project manager at Rocha Enterprises. The Turtle Tear renovation is mine!

One

Three months later...

The club is packed. Bodies grind together on the dance floor. There's barely room to move. You catch my eye.

You're alone.

Bass pounds through my body, rushes from my head to my toes, takes the same path your eyes follow. Your dark-eyed stare is flutter-soft on my skin. It raises goose bumps. Makes me flush. My vodka and cranberry-soaked blood runs hot with need.

You smile. Dimples pierce your cheeks. Your eyes flash. I can't resist.

"Rach!" Shannon grabs my arm. She's sweaty from dancing and pulls her blonde hair up off her shoulders. "I'm going." She tilts her head toward Shawn or Shane or Seth—I'm not sure—the guy she met two hours ago.

"How am I supposed to get home?" She drove.

Shannon shoves her car keys in my hand. "See you in the morning." She winks and pushes back through the crowd toward the guy whose name starts with an S.

When I turn from watching Shannon go, you're standing right in front of me. "Hi," you say. Familiarity strikes, but I don't think I'd ever forget meeting you.

"Hi." I fall into your dark eyes and can't get out. They're serious and focused on mine. Looking away would be a crime.

You run a hand through your wavy black-brown hair. Are you nervous? I can't tell. "What were you drinking?" You tap my glass, empty except for melting ice.

"Vodka and cranberry." I take in a thick, damp breath. Dancing bodies fog up the air, make it heavy to breathe.

You shake your beer bottle, indicating its emptiness. "I'm headed to the bar. Would you like another?"

I have to drive Shannon's car home, but I don't want to stop talking to you. I nod. "Please." I'll drink slowly. I'll drive even slower.

I follow behind you, taking in the view of your incredible backside in jeans. A black long-sleeved shirt shifts with your strong, wide shoulders and hugs your narrow waist. You work out. *A lot.* The body I'm staring at didn't come from luck and a good gene pool.

You glance back to make sure I'm following. When a group of people push between us, you reach out and take my hand. My fingers curl around yours like they're possessed.

We reach the bar. You squeeze between two men. I stand back to wait while you order. I watch you reach into your pocket. A second later, you turn to me and hand me a glass.

"Thanks." I take a deep drink, ignoring my self-promise to sip and make it last. Looking at you, I need all the courage this vodka is offering.

You sip your beer, watching me. An intense magnetism pulls between us. I'm sweating. I wipe my forehead with the back of my hand. The vodka is kicking in fast. I stumble sideways. You grip my arm.

"Feeling okay?" you ask.

The room spins and tilts. Black spots swim through my vision. "No. I need to sit." My drink slips through my fingers and splatters on my bare leg.

"I've got you." You put an arm around me and lead me toward the door. "You need some air."

I'm blacking out and coming to, over and over again. This has never happened from three and a half vodka and cranberries before. "I need to get home."

"I'll take you," you say.

"No. I . . ." The words won't come. They buzz around in the darkness inside my mind searching for the light. I watch them break apart and fade.

You usher me through the parking lot. Open the door of a black car. Put me inside. "We'll be home soon," you say, buckling a seatbelt around my waist.

I try to grip the door handle to get out. My arm won't move. My head lulls on my shoulder. The blackness narrows, leaving a small tunnel focused on the dashboard. Then it closes completely.

No more words.

No more light.

No more sound.

Just like that—I'm taken.